THE RANGERS

BLAZE WARD

Knotted Road Press

CONTENTS

ALSO BY BLAZE WARD

The Jessica Keller Chronicles

Auberon

Queen of the Pirates

Last of the Immortals

Goddess of War

Flight of the Blackbird

Additional Alexandria Station Stories

The Story Road

Siren

The Science Officer Series

The Science Officer

The Mind Field

The Gilded Cage

The Pleasure Dome

The Doomsday Vault

The Last Flagship

The Hammerfield Gambit

The Hammerfield Payoff

Doyle Iwakuma Stories

The Librarian

Demigod

Greater Than The Gods Intended

Other Science Fiction Stories

Myrmidons

Moonshot

Menelaus

Earthquake Gun

Moscow Gold

Fairchild

White Crane

The *Collective* Universe

The Shipwrecked Mermaid

Imposters

FOREWORD

Who will resist? Who will stand?

These core questions ensure history is not simply a litany of the conquered and the conquerors, the oppressed and the oppressors, but will also include those who tell the unforgettable stories of the ones who pushed back against the coming darkness. Those who resisted being conquered.

Be it a rocky cliff face at Thermopylae, an adobe mission named the Alamo, or Sitting Bull in the American West, our history is peppered with resistance. Not all who resisted bore guns. The names of Ghandi and Martin Luther King rest as firmly in the history books as that of Winston Churchill.

What history remembers are those who pushed back against the inevitable tide in the name of truth and right.

But history is the past. There will be need for new heroes in our coming age. More people that, when faced with opposition, will rely on a belief of an inherent debt to their fellow man to fuel their resolve.

And just such a new power has arrived. In November of 2016, Donald J. Trump became the President-elect of the United States of America. An unbelievable dream for some for whom access to riches of the land, until then shielded by government and citizens for future generations, was a relentless objective. And, for others who found him to be the new face of evil, it was a nightmare.

Those who considered his ascension to be an unthinkable horror had their fears confirmed when plans for scaling back environmental protections were revealed.

In the face of this new dynamic, an unlikely band of heroes across the American West rose to defend the birthright of a nation so that it might be passed to future generations. The US Park Service. They tweeted. They blogged. They said, "No." They stood firm. And we cheered.

It is from this present that the future is born in the brilliant mind of Blaze Ward. He found the unlikely heroes of his future history and he set them to riding the ridges in the divided and shattered land that had once been America, to guard the frontier against new invasions and tyranny.

Stand for us in heart and soul, his heroes, his Rangers do. Under Blaze's steady pen, these Rangers don the badge of service and bring the spirit of the West, as Louis Lamour would have loved but never imagined.

I invite you to read and love these stories of victory, defeat, and struggle, each told in a way that reveals strength of character, from those who base their service to the country and the land it occupies on values passed down for generations.

Blaze Ward's rangers provide hope for the future.

Bob Brown
Richland, WA
2017

THE LAST RANGER

D ale looked over at the old man in the green jacket next to him and considered how the world had gotten here.

Not just them, sitting here on horseback. Two men in a semi-blizzard.

Everything.

Martial law hadn't been the first step. Nor the last.

They said it started back in the middle somewhere, when hope was still an option. Before some idiot decided the best way to break the back of the Resistance was to use *The Bomb*.

Even people in favor of nuking LA in those days had decided that was a bridge too far. Everything went to hell at that point. Flyover country became a foreign land.

Still was.

Everyone argued over who got to keep the name *United States of America*, but the two sides generally settled into *Blue Shirts* and *Green Shirts* as a way of telling people apart, at least in conversation.

Stan still sat tall in the well-worn saddle after thirty-five years as a Park Ranger. Legend had it he was the last man authorized under the old United States Congress to wear the golden shield with the buffalo. When he was only a few years older than Dale was now.

Back before.

Before war, and apocalypse, and ruin. Before it was assumed that a sixteen-year-old like Dale would grow up and become a warrior.

Stan was staring hard into his binoculars, intent on something in the distance occasionally obscured by the cold, blowing wind that whipped at the two men and caused their horses' manes to fly out flat to the horizon.

Only fools and Park Rangers had any business out in weather like this, but it was January, and they had patrol rounds to finish.

Dale grabbed his Dewar flask from the left hand saddle bag and took a gulp of honeyed tea, still hot, hours since they'd broken camp. Stan remained still as an old rock outcropping, so Dale put the flask away and made sure no snow had gotten into his rifle holster. He double-checked that his outer gear was all buttoned up and dry.

When they were out in the open field, a team like theirs had to carry almost everything they needed on the move, from food, to medical gear, to explosives for starting a controlled avalanche. It was all tightly packed in oversized saddle bags. Everything might be individually light, but there was still a lot of it, spread between the two horses.

Just in case, he made sure that his horse, Centurion, was holding up.

All good.

Father's lessons had been hammered home over Dale's short lifetime. If he wanted to be a warrior when he grew up, a Park Ranger, here were all the things he was expected to master. And he had.

At sixteen, Dale was already an Apprentice Guide, an *090*, assigned to work with the Old Man of the Service himself.

Royalty.

Stan muttered something rude under his breath.

Dale had learned stillness and silence from his father while hunting mountain goats in these Rockies. He waited for the man to share.

"Trouble," the quiet veteran finally said, handing Dale the binoculars.

Dale took long moments to get the focus on the binoculars back down where he needed it. Stan's eyes were going, but his nose for trouble was still unmatched in the Service.

Movement. Gray and green against the mostly white and black background. Dale dialed the focus down tighter.

Tanks waddling slowly through the snowbanks far below them, cutting a trail. Troop transports, similar tracked, armored beasts behind that. Articulated vehicles on treads as well. A convoy of them. Maybe a dozen, total.

Most of that armor were antiques these days. Relics from

the old United States Army, stored in some depot when the world fell apart and then rehabilitated into service today.

Dale lowered the glasses and considered the terrain. Colorado and Wyoming were both on the Green side, but the eastern portions of both states were flat and open. Easy enough for Jayhawkers and Huskers, Kansas and Nebraska Guard Units, to sneak over the line. Especially if they came across the old Pawnee Prairie in the kind of blizzard that had been blowing the last few days.

No roads. Lots of flat. Nothing to stop the wind or raiders.

Slice the gap between Fort Collins and Cheyenne. Cut south of Virginia Dale and pass the old abandoned Benedictine Abbey. Sneak into the mountains before anybody knew they were there.

What the hell did they want?

He turned back to Stan, found the old man watching him like a hawk. Waiting.

"So Red Feather Lakes Road is watched," Dale began. "And Highway Fourteen and Thirty-Four are pretty heavily fortified. Why are they coming in this way?"

"What's there to hit?" Stan asked. "That's enough there to do some damage, wherever they decide to land."

"I suppose you could cut off Eighty," Dale replied. "Or maybe fortify the reservoir. Or even poison it. I didn't see any air cover, but the clouds would block us anyway."

Dale stopped and turned his head the other direction. Mountains covered in snow, as far as the eye could see.

"And I supposed helicopters or low-flying attack planes would give them away," he continued, working out the logic aloud, like he was being graded. He probably was. "So either they want to set up a base deep in the hills, like a tick waiting for spring, or they are a blocking force sent to cut off reinforcements if someone is going to attack Fort Collins."

Sun Tzu had covered this sort of thing. So had Patton. Dale had read both several times growing up. Dad had a whole library.

Stan nodded. Somehow, he conveyed approval and respect with a simple bob of the head.

"Is there any advantage to poisoning the reservoir?" Stan asked.

Yeah, Dale was being graded today.

"Panic," Dale replied. "But actually doing it would risk an escalation from one of the other nations surrounding the Blues. Still, you could get people moving south to Denver in the middle of a raid and winter. But why come this way? It's easier to come into the reservoir from the east if you want to hit it. So that's out. I'd want to hide someplace farther west, where there are more trees."

Stan nodded again.

"So would I," he agreed.

Dale thought he would say something else, but Stan just whipped Audrey's reins and got the big, bay mare moving. Centurion had spent enough time in the Park Service to follow without any heels. The blue roan was big, and occasionally a goof, but he was a soldier, too.

Dale let Stan set the pace, pushing through the snow toward some target to the southwest.

Between them, they had two rifles and two pistols. Plus two cavalry sabers.

That force over there had a couple of tanks, half a dozen armored transports, and probably a hundred men in battle gear. In back, several flatbeds were hauling covered loads Dale couldn't identify.

Trouble.

And near as Dale knew, there were no friendly troops this side of Fort Collins that could help.

Dale wasn't sure how they could stop them, but he knew Stan was dead set on trying.

———

They ended up in a stand of trees on the east side of Turkey Roost Mountain, still deep in the heart of what used to be the Roosevelt forest. He and Stan were down below the peak, just lee enough that the howling wind was quiet here, but Dale could still see the angry edges of the storm running on all sides of them.

The west face was where the North Fork River would run hard and dangerous in the spring melt, but for now, it was ice. Over here, just the least amount of gully and enough trees that they could hang a camouflage net and settle the horses in a bit.

Dale glanced back over his left shoulder as the sun began to set.

Or would have set, if it was visible. More snow was coming.

He wasn't sure if another storm would slow down those Jayhawkers. It would certainly provide them enough cover to do mischief, up here in the mountains.

Stan had called for backup, but it just confirmed that there was nobody within range.

Made sense. If this was cover for an attack on Fort Collins, they would need everybody down in the flats.

Still, it would have been nice to have some help out here.

They started a climb, letting Audrey and Centurion hump along at a nice amble. The two horses had fought hard to get them here early enough, but they still had a bit to go before everyone was done.

"There's only one way we might slow them down," Stan said in that quiet drawl. "Stop them, maybe."

Dale nodded. There wasn't a lot two men with rifles could do against an armored company in rough country.

Die, maybe, but Stan wasn't a Death or Glory kind of guy. Not today, anyway.

Stan took his silence with a nod.

"Assuming they want to stay off Eighty as much as possible, they should pass below us," Stan said. "We can ambush them here, and then run like hell for the back country and hope they don't catch us."

"They've got tanks, Stan," Dale felt compelled to point out the obvious.

The old man actually grinned at that.

"Those are nice in an open field, kid," he replied. "Ain't worth shit in tight quarters. And those guns only elevate so far. No, I'd be much more worried if they had horses with them, or snow-mobiles. This gives us a chance."

They were still fifty-ton behemoths, invulnerable to anything at hand. Dale wasn't about to point that out. Again.

"And the troop transports?" Dale asked instead.

"Man on foot in this snow is about as worthless as tits on a boar, Dale," Stan said. "Only thing I worry about is aircraft, but the snow'll be too much."

Dale nodded.

He'd never fired his rifle in anger, unless you counted being pissed off at an elk that zigged when it should have zagged, two winters ago, and would've gotten away, if his dad hadn't drilled it. His dad was like that.

But there were Blues coming. Lots of them. As Stan had said, this was enough force to do something stupid with, if the commander over there had a mind to.

Dale wondered if the man had ever read Sun Tzu, or Patton. Rommel. Wellington. Light Horse Harry Lee. Any of them.

It would be a man. Blues didn't allow women to serve. Feared that it would somehow sully their delicate womanliness. Taint their femininity.

Dale's mom had been a drill instructor, once upon a time. There wasn't anything delicate about that woman but her drop biscuits.

The top of Turkey Roost was a bald knob of gray granite, slicked over with what little snow and ice could hang on in the teeth of that bitter northwest wind coming down.

Stan directed Dale to tie the horses loosely to a tree, part of a stand down on a little shoulder, something that would provide them some cover and a wind break. Assuming nobody decided to fly overhead anytime soon and maybe catch them moving about on an infrared scanner.

And even that would get muddled up by the wind and snowfall coming at them. They might look like deer.

Stan had found a tree and settled into the lee of it. Every little bit to block the wind, especially up here where there was no cover at all. Dale fell into his lee, kneeling down and letting his chaps and boots protect his knees from the cold stone.

The Ranger had his optics out, but Dale's eyes were good enough to see the Jayhawks coming. They had chosen to come up Mill Creek instead of the North Fork. Flip of a coin which was smarter.

Dale was still surprised at the raid. All he could think of was that this was a supply column being escorted into the wilderness, to hide a stash depot in advance of the spring offensive. Nothing else made any sense, especially as valuable as those vehicle had to be.

Even over the wind, those ancient turbines screamed like angry raptors. Long column of beasts, coming closer.

Dale would have said wolves, but the Jayhawks were exactly backward from that. Wolves put the weak and old up front to set the pace, so nobody got left behind, with the Alpha at the very rear.

Buffalo, maybe.

These yahoos had both tanks up front, followed by about half of the troop transports, creeping along slowly and crushing small trees and squishing the snow down so the big, articulated trucks in back had a clear trail. As long as they stayed mostly on the bank, everything would be fine.

Dale had studied enough history of the old days to know those tanks down there were really low-flying spaceships, bundled up tight with their own air, heat, and radios. Nobody had made any new tanks in maybe twenty-five years, since folks had started sabotaging the factories that made the war machines, but both sides had inherited thousands of the old beasts from the United States Army, back when it was a thing, and not the degenerate street gang they were witnessing today.

Patton would have cried. Or slapped someone.

"Final exam, Dale," Stan announced in a voice that brooked

no sass. "They will pass below us in column. I have explosives enough to bring down a significant portion of that overhanging shelf of rock. What timing do we seek?"

Dale nodded, mostly as a placeholder.

They were on the top of Turkey Roost Mountain, looking down from a sheer cliff face, a wall running at an angle to the valley below where the stone went straight down nearly twenty meters before it flattened out again. They could drop an avalanche, not just of snow, but of tons and tons of mountain as well.

That much was obvious. But that wasn't the question Stan was asking.

This man was a legend. The Last Ranger of the National Park Service, from the time before Blue and Green.

From the old world, before Park Rangers were the police force of the west, protecting the wilderness and the people from the Robber Barons and the Drumphers.

When they were just teachers, and not paladins.

What timing do we seek?

It was a question with a blade hidden in the folds of the fabric, as Musashi would have summarized it. Sun Tzu would have nodded with the swordmaster.

Larimer County was all rippled up, waves of rock frozen forever, leaving troughs where ticks and Jayhawks could hide.

At the same time, it wasn't like the leading face down by Denver, where artillery on the hills could range damned-near forever, and you had to climb hard up the few passable places, channeled into killzones designed by sadists with history degrees.

You couldn't just stop the Jayhawkers by dropping the rocks now. That was the obvious trap. The raiders would just go around you. Maybe backtrack down the North Fork a mile or so and circle around Turkey Roost to come up the back, like he and Stan had done.

Tanks in relatively open country would chase them down like a pack of wolves on a lone buffalo calf.

No, you had to drop the rock and snow *on* them. Avalanche

the stone down atop the snake and trap it. Immobilize them here, so that later reinforcements could come roll them up, after whatever was going to happen that these yahoos were here for in the first place.

Patton smiled at him with a cruel eye. Wellington spoke to him of Salamanca.

Stan had asked a different question.

How many men did Dale want to kill today?

None. He had joined the Park Service and not the army because he wanted to help people. He wasn't a killer.

But this was war. They were Jayhawks.

"They likely to stop for the night, anytime soon?" Dale asked.

Laagers would be better defended, but easier to mousetrap. Rommel reminded him of the Battle of Caporetto, before he was famous, but still a genius.

Stan glanced back at the western sky.

"Horse troop would have, already," Stan said, but Dale knew that. "Armor doesn't need to, as long as they have fuel and maps. Two of those big rigs are hauling jet fuel for the machines."

Ah. That's what those were.

There were a pair of them, tucked in at the front of the others. Dale had wondered if they were mobile missile launchers of some sort. Articulated, armored canteens on treads made more sense.

"How come we don't have tanks up here?" Dale asked.

It didn't really matter. Inspiration had lit up his mind, followed by the sound of both the Iron Duke and Light Horse Harry laughing maniacally.

They did that.

Killing was generally wrong, but there were times when it was the best of a set of bad choices. Dale had never had to confront that until today.

People were likely to die as a result of his choices.

He swallowed past a dry tongue and listened.

"Too easy to bomb fuel depots," Stan replied. "Even way out

on the west coast. Blues still have an Air Force, even if we got the Springs in the divorce. Plus, too damned rough up here. Figure they'll have to fix at least one major breakdown before they get wherever they want to end up."

Dale nodded carefully, that plan's shape crystalizing.

"In the southwest and in the spring, they always say you cut off the head of the snake," he observed.

He'd never been to Arizona, now mostly empty land and Indian reservation, once all the Snowbirds had gone East during the first war. It hadn't been India and Pakistan Partitioning, but there had still been long convoys in and out of Texas, once things got serious.

Mom had served there, before she had met dad. Still had a magnificent thunderbird tattoo across her back as a reminder.

Stan watched him, utterly motionless.

"Hopefully, we won't have to kill too many of them," Dale continued in a low voice. "But they should have stayed in Kansas, so they need to be batted on the nose with a rolled up newspaper. Maybe next time, they'll think twice and stay home."

Stan grinned.

He stood and tucked the optics back into their case. Dale stood as well.

"When I was a kid," Stan laughed, "this would be the point where someone says: *Here, hold my beer.*"

Dale wasn't sure what that phrase meant, but the cold, steel gleam in Stan's eyes gave him some clue about how dangerous it was about to become.

Dale had never played with high explosives. Sure, there had been familiarization classes with plastic explosives and recoilless rifles, still the best way to knock down avalanches under controlled circumstances.

But he had never really gotten to play with the squishy stuff.

Still hadn't, technically. Stan had done all the work, cramming cold globs down into four ice-filled crevices, always careful not to slip and fly. The snow might be thick and soft below, but you were still going to be falling far enough to break bones at the very best.

In this weather, probably a slow, painful death, especially when that vale turned into a battlefield in a little while.

The column of angry buffalo was still creeping along, but not much faster than a man could walk. Which made sense, with fifty tons of tank; deep snow; small, frozen rivers; and no scouts out front on horses.

It was slow work.

No radios. Detonators on long wires that Dale was holding, back up and in the trees, as Stan worked below him. The twist-plunger was sitting next to Dale.

Stan had explained how to wire it and set everything off, in case he died out there, but Dale was content to wait. Hopefully, all he would do today is watch, but he had a feeling that Stan was going to make him do the killing.

If you wanted to join the Park Service and become a Ranger, those were the costs. Others would be happy to stay as *189*'s or *303*'s, Recreation Aides and Clerks, but Dale was already an apprentice Guide, an *090*, and had his heart set on becoming an *025*, a true *Park Ranger*, with the gold badge and buffalo embroidered on his shoulder.

Warrior.

Stan pushed another glob of gray evil into a hole at his feet and stuffed a wire down, like a long-tail sperm cell just penetrating an egg to give birth to fire.

The sky lit up with the sound of thunder. Which made no sense. Wasn't the right kind of storm for thundersnow.

Wasn't thunder.

Someone had opened up with a machine gun.

Blues had suddenly realized they weren't alone up here in the great, peaceful wilderness.

Stan flipped up in the air suddenly, turned a complete somersault, and face-planted in the snow.

Dale was about a hundred feet away, but he could see blood starting to stain the snow.

And Stan wasn't moving.

Dale lurched to his feet and stopped.

Their job was to stop the Blues. Paralyze them. Nail them to the ground like a catfish on a board, waiting to be cleaned for dinner.

There was nothing he could do for the man if Stan was dead. And the blues were ripping the sky with tracer rounds, turning the twilight purple and pink.

Someone had seen Stan move, on the ridge above them. And nailed him pretty good.

But they thought there were more people around.

A dragon roared, like Gabriel sounding his horn.

Dale watched a one-twenty-five round from the leading tank slam into the far hillside, across the vale and down a half-mile. He didn't know if it was paranoia pulling the trigger, or an unlucky rabbit coming out to feed.

Didn't matter.

Something had drawn their attention. More dragons bellowed, drowning out the baying of angry wolves throwing bullets in every direction.

It was like watching God himself fire a shotgun out of the sky, seeing the snow erupt in little puffs as bullets and explosions went every which way.

Dale was frozen with fear. He forced himself to breathe.

Even Centurion was better trained for this sort of thing than he was.

"Blow it, kid," Stan's voice was suddenly there above the din.

Dale looked over.

Stan was lying in a pool of blood, staining the snow bright crimson.

Even from here, Dale could see the old man gritting his teeth in pain, that precipice not too far beyond him.

"Get out of there, Stan," Dale yelled back.

Stan shook his head.

"Can't move," he hollered over the ongoing gunfire.

"I'll rescue you," Dale almost pleaded.

Those angry, blue eyes speared Dale's soul from clear over there.

"Do your duty, Ranger," Stan commanded.

Dale understood.

He fought back the tears and kneeled, as if in prayer.

Or, also in prayer.

There was a whole package of plastic explosives in that cliff face, just waiting for Joshua.

Dale pulled off his gloves like Stan had showed him. Frostbite was always a risk doing this, but a small one. Better to handle the wires under fingertips than mittens and gloves.

Dale pulled a knife to cut and strip the ends of the wires. He opened the wingnuts and wrapped the four wires tight on the poles.

Something whoomped like an ominous kettle drum. Dale damned near peed himself, until the mortar round landed up-valley in a blast of submunitions and explosives. Vicious, little baseballs of doom and ugliness shredding the snow and trees.

There were a lot of scared kids right below him, just from the sound of gunfire.

And one scared kid up here.

Dale fixed his eyes on Stan and unlocked the plunger. It opened under his hands with a half twist.

Stan nodded, calm as a man at Sunday morning service.

All the tears were Dale's.

Another deep breath.

He nodded back at the old man, the Last Ranger, and twisted the handle down.

Hell came to earth.

Fire, and brimstone, and Lucifer himself, near as Dale could tell.

The earth itself moved amidst all the fire, knocking Dale on his ass. The plunger dropped into the snow next to him, fallen from numb hands.

Half the mountain looked like it was gone, four giant bites

taken out of the face, like an angry mole the size of a whale had been there.

Silence, too.

All the firing had stopped, like a Christmas Day Armistice. There had been a song about that.

Dale picked himself up and crept forward, unsure how safe the rocks were, now that someone had taken a ballpeen sledge to them.

It looked safer to the right, so he moved that way. Just enough to peek over.

There was a snake down there, all right. A big one. Mighty angry.

Dale had dropped a bigger rock on top of it.

It took a moment to resolve. Dale hadn't realized just how much mountain was down there now.

Way more than he had been expecting.

The avalanche of snow and stone had hit the snake just about in the middle. Right where Light Horse Harry had suggested.

Half the troop transports were buried, because Dale had blown it earlier than he planned, but he had still gotten the two tankers, buried them under tons of rock and yards of snow.

Like Harry had said. Horse will graze just fine on grass. Tanks don't have that option. No silage, no cavalry.

Everyone had stopped firing down there.

Probably shock. Sure as hell a goodly amount of surprise.

Who expected someone to drop a mountain on them?

Wouldn't last that long.

Dale crept back out of sight before anybody saw him. The tanks could still move, so he needed to get gone, but there was no way in hell he was coming home with Audrey and not Stan.

Crazed patterns of stress had lit up these rocks, like a china plate glued back together.

Stan was still in the middle of it, so Dale moved as carefully as he could.

It was still a long ways down, and that cliff was a lot closer than it had been.

Stan was on his back when Dale got close. Probably flipped by all the shockwaves that had knocked Dale on his own ass.

There wasn't much time, and Stan wasn't all that heavy, regardless of heavy, winter clothing. Tall and wiry come summer greens. Dale knelt at his side and felt for a pulse. He could easily throw the old man's body into a fireman's carry and get him to cover.

"Hold my beer," Stan murmured.

Dale was so shocked he fell on his butt again.

"Aren't you supposed to be dead?" Dale asked as he got back up.

"Ya gotta know how to play with high explosives, kid," Stan explained. "Shaping charges is an art form."

"Can you walk?" Dale asked, standing and offering a hand. "We need to be somewhere else."

Stan took the hand and let Dale pull him up, his left arm hanging useless by his side.

Dale grabbed a handful of snow and pushed it into the bloody hole in Stan's shoulder.

All Dad's first aid lessons came back as he did. Hit just right and there's nothing but muscle and bone to hurt. Below the tendons, above the lungs, miss the heart. Pretty survivable wound.

He turned Stan around and stuffed more snow into the back.

Dying by Blue was a bigger risk than shock and blood loss right now. Those folks would be angry and vicious, at least until their commander got them under control and figured out what had happened.

And what they could do now, with the snake chopped right in half.

Audrey and Centurion could get the two of them far enough away that Dale could sew the old man up and get more teams vectored in. Or watch from a really safe distance while some idiots went full frontal on Fort Collins, expecting a flank surprise that had just gotten its teeth kicked in.

Dale got Stan down to the horses and boosted the old man up onto Audrey's saddle with a shoulder under his ass.

Centurion held perfectly still, and then turned and took point all by himself, like he recognized that Audrey needed to walk careful going home.

They were both better at this than he was.

"You done good, kid," Stan said through gritted teeth. "No. You done good, Ranger."

"But I'm only an *090*, Stan," Dale argued. "A Guide."

"No, Dale," Stan said firmly. "After today, you're a Ranger."

THE MAIDEN

By the time that blizzard had finally broken, Dale had stitched up Stan's shoulder about as well as it could be done, using the half-moon needle with the silk thread. It was a clean bullet wound, in and out with only Stan's collar bone snapped.

Medevac VTOL had dropped out of the clouds at that point, loading the old man up and dropping off a replacement Ranger, fellow named Wilson who spoke about as few words as a human could get by with.

Stan's bay mare, Audrey, was spooked by losing her favorite rider, so Dale ended up riding her, and putting Wilson on his horse, Centurion. The blue roan was a little grumpy, but Dale managed to soothe the big goof by talking. Wilson had a firm hand, and was soft about it.

Both horses settled down after thirty minutes or so.

"Hawkins said to treat you like a Ranger," Wilson said out of the blue.

Dale wasn't so sure about that.

Sure, Stan had said he was a Ranger now, one of the elite warriors of the National Park Service. And Stan's word went a long ways with the Service. He was, according to legend, the last Ranger authorized under the old United States government. The last man to wear the gold badge with the buffalo.

Before Drumph. Before martial law and the breakdown.

Before the radioactive crater that used to be Los Angeles.

Dale shrugged by way of answering. Wasn't his call.

Wilson wouldn't be offended by his silence. Most folks would need to talk. To defend themselves.

But Park Rangers tended to be a taciturn bunch.

Words didn't matter. Not out here in the North Colorado Rockies and the Roosevelt Forest.

Deeds.

Nothing more. Nothing less.

Nothing else.

Dale would have liked to have headed home after they got Stan clear, but it was January, and they still had patrol rounds to finish.

At least he didn't have to watch the convoy of Jayhawk tanks and trucks that had tried to sneak into the mountains. Between Stan dropping a mountain on their convoy, well, Dale, but Stan had done most of the work, and the blizzard; them Kansas boys had been more than happy to surrender when another Park Ranger had walked into their camp and asked politely.

The alternative would have been walking near a hundred miles through blizzard piles to get back to Nebraska, as the closest border. Even more to get back to Kansas.

Not even spring would get some of those troop transports loose.

Dale caught Wilson studying him sidelong.

At least the man was grinning. Dale grinned back.

"You'll do, kid," Wilson decided.

Dale hoped so. He was just an *090*, a Guide, while both Stan and Wilson were *025*'s, Park Service Rangers.

Those were big shoes to fill for a sixteen-year-old.

<hr>

W ilson had offered to help him with the horses, when they finally got back to barracks, but Dale preferred to do the work himself. Even Stan had stopped by, his left arm was in a sling where he had no business currying a horse right now.

Plus Audrey was still freaked out.

Not as much as Dale, but still.

It felt good to take care of both horses personally, instead of leaving it for one of the grooms.

Centurion had his nose pressed against the bars separating stalls, indignant that Dale was paying attention to someone other than him. Even if it was only Audrey.

Dale's horse was a dork, somedays.

'Nother shadow darkened the stall door as Dale worked.

Thin, weedy. Maybe five foot six. Dale felt like a giant, half a head taller.

Man had an elegant mustache, though, and a degree in accounting from the Colorado School of Mines. Qualified him to be a Superintendent, even if he came from the *303* side of things.

Anyone that didn't carry a gun in the field had started out as a *303* at some point. Even the lawyers.

"I've read Stan Hawkins' report, Embry," Superintendent Azad began.

He had a deep voice, but it still managed to sound thin.

Dale nodded, looking over Audrey's back as he brushed the bay mare down.

"He recommended that you be promoted from *090* to *025*," Azad continued forcefully. "Were you aware of that?"

Again, Dale nodded. Dad had taught him the importance of silence as a weapon with people that liked the sound of their own voice. Hilar Azad was a man like that.

"And your opinion?" Azad finally asked.

"Not my call, Superintendent," Dale replied in that quiet, respectful voice that Dad had taught him, and Stan had reinforced, when he wanted people to actually listen.

Azad harrumphed disdainfully.

"Is that all you have to say?"

Dale fixed him with a hard glare. Audrey seemed to understand the situation and stood stock still.

"My goal is to become a Park Ranger, Superintendent Azad," Dale replied. "Got no timeframe on getting there. Plan to serve for decades, Good Lord willing."

"So you think you deserve it?" Azad sneered.

Dale let the man's superiority roll off him like water off a duck.

"We serve because we can," Dale echoed both his father and Stan Hawkins, men he respected. "Man after glory got no place in the Park Service. Let him join the fire department and smoke jump."

Azad's eyes got narrow, but he held his peace.

Centurion snorted in the silence, but that doofus barely understood what the reins were for. He wasn't listening to the men talk.

Audrey, maybe she understood. The mare was smarter than she let on with most folk.

"You're too young to be an *025*, Embry," Azad decided. "But I've put you in for a medal for your heroism."

"Thank you, sir," Dale nodded at Azad's back as he left abruptly.

About what he had been expecting. Not that it carried much truck.

The only thing that really mattered around the men he respected was that gold badge with the buffalo in the center.

And he'd get there, one of these days.

Stan had been a ranger for nigh on thirty-five years now.

And it wasn't like the war would likely be over, anytime soon.

G uides didn't rate private quarters, so Dale was in a quad, dozing on a bottom bunk. Three other young men in here were dead to the world around him.

Sun wasn't due up for another couple of hours, but he wasn't really asleep. Out in the field, now'd be about the time to roust and start building up the fire for morning tea and hotcakes.

Those habits had been hammered into him for more than a decade by this point.

The door opened on nearly silent hinges.

"You up?" Wilson asked in a quiet tone.

"Yeah," Dale said, tossing the blanket back and sitting up.

Like many of the old-timers who had taught him, Dale slept dressed, even in the barracks. You never knew when you would need to move quick-like in an emergency. Best not be naked, fighting that fire.

Feet went into boots before they hit the floor. Suspenders went up over the shoulders, pulled taut as he stood. Dale grabbed his jacket from the hook at the foot of the frame.

Wilson stepped back onto the porch wearing a grin as Dale

approached. He was a big man. Six and a half feet tall. Broad shoulders. V-chest.

Like most of the Park Rangers, scrawny, bowed legs held him up. Dale still ran and lifted weights to keep his lower strong. You never knew when you'd have to walk twenty miles out, either.

Dale pulled the door shut behind him with a quiet click and nodded to the man.

Wilson was in his mid-forties, so he had about three decades on Dale. About half of that had been an *025*, and the man was as quiet as he was respected.

"I'm covering Hawkins' Patrol Area 'til he heals," Wilson began, his breath steaming in the partial light of the permanent barracks. "Was hopin' you were up for joining me."

"You're a Ranger," Dale said. "I'm just a Guide. You can issue orders."

"Sup' might think you're only a Guide, kid," Wilson replied. "I'll take Hawkins' opinion, any day."

"I'm yours, Ranger," Dale said.

Wilson grinned at him in a lop-sided way.

"Let's ride."

Pronto was already saddled up when they got to the barn.

Dale still thought she was about the weirdest-looking horse he'd ever seen, but she was also one of the nicest. Liver chestnut coat on her top half, never black but never that far away; splashed white bottom, like she'd forded a river just deep enough to walk, and had washed every bit of color out of her hide when she did. Including her head, which was white almost to the eyes, like she'd been drinking from that river, too.

If they could have reversed it, she'd disappear in all this snow. As it was, she'd look like she was flying across it, even standing still. Probably thought she was, too.

Pronto was like that, even with Wilson.

Centurion had obviously gotten over his anger. He was right there when Dale approached the groom holding him. Stood perfectly still when the saddle went on, instead of his usual dancing and nipping. Only wiggled his butt once to settle the saddle bags and rifle holder.

Dale and Wilson did the ritual of checking out rifles and pistols, inspecting each and loading them while the other called the quiet cadence, step by step down the checklist of gear and location. That ritual that covered all the little things a Ranger had to do.

Little habits ingrained early that were the ones that saved your life.

Sabers went opposite the rifles. Overcoats got buttoned up. Scarves got wound tight. Hats got crammed down with draw-strings snug, Wilson in his Ranger hat, Dale wearing an old beaver cowboy hat handed down from his grandfather.

Points went into stirrups, butts went onto saddles, horses practically danced over to the main gate.

Ranger of the Guard checked them off on an old-fashioned clip-board as she nodded to one of her men for the gate to open.

"Wilson and Embry, headed out for Patrol," she called in the morning dimness.

She saluted. Dale and Wilson saluted back.

Dale figured he'd probably catch hell, if Azad ever caught wind.

Only a Ranger headed out rated a call. Technically, she should have said "Ranger Wilson, headed out for Patrol."

Another one who would listen to Stan over the Superintendent.

Weren't much Dale could do about it but keep his head down and his nose clean.

"That's does not look right," Dale muttered aloud, pulling Centurion's reins just enough to stop the big oaf with nothing more than a little sideways tapdance.

Calm for the roan.

Pronto came to rest as well. She obviously didn't feel the need to show off today.

Wilson eloquently raised a single eyebrow above the scarf covering the bottom half of his face. Always a man of few words.

Dale considered the rifle in the holster for a second, but settled for touching the pistol at his hip. Good, old-fashioned, .45 Long Colt, firing modern rounds: lead, around a copper hollow-point core, with a steel nail in the middle. Run through any barrel. Kill anything less than a bear. Punch right through kelvar, even as it broke ribs.

He grabbed the reins and dismounted to inspect the snow.

Blizzard a week ago had dropped another four to six inches of snow, and it hadn't warmed at all, so the stuff was still mostly powder.

But for a weird-looking pattern that came out of the trees on the right and disappeared down a swale to the left.

Regular-like.

Unnatural.

Light Horse Harry Lee, First American Revolution General, tapped him on the shoulder and pointed. Dale shifted his feet. George S. Patton laughed.

"I'll be damned," Dale said, standing. "Bells on bobbed tails."

"Kid?" Wilson asked.

Dale turned to grin up at the man.

"So suppose you had a two horse rig," Dale began. "Hauling a sledge or a sleigh with three rails."

Wilson squinted, visualizing things.

"That would leave a nice, clean trail through this forest, wouldn't it?" Dale asked

The Ranger nodded.

"Now suppose you hooked a board or something behind you on a couple of chains," Dale continued. "With tines hanging off the back of that, like a leaf rake, to break up the snow and fluff it back up after you crunched it down. Betcha that snow would look a lot like this."

"Slow running," Wilson stated.

"And damned hard to recognize," Dale said, thinking like a

Guide was supposed to. "Maybe a day ago. Two more days or another snow and it would have just vanished."

"Recommendation?" Wilson asked.

"Hey," Dale countered, climbing back onto Centurion's back. "You're the Ranger."

"Funny, kid."

Wilson flicked his reins and turned Pronto's head to follow the tracks

Dale whickered at the blue roan and followed.

Just another day in the Park Service.

"Not sure we should both go down there," Dale hazarded. Guides were supposed to follow orders, but Wilson and Stan both treated him like an equal.

This might be the one time he would actually tread that ice.

Wilson glanced over, jaw jutting just so.

Another man might have actually spoken.

Down there was their rabbit.

A modern-looking sledge, built from metal and fiberglass, rather than wood. Three rails, which would make the ride hell, even on springs, but would probably stabilize it much better on rough terrain.

Damn thing had still flipped when the driver caught a hidden rock with the right rail as he hit a drop with the left.

Horses looked a little beat up, but at least the frame had torn mostly loose, so they hadn't been drug under with the thing.

Dale pulled out his binoculars to look.

Sure enough, driver was hanging halfway out from under the shell.

Looked dead.

Nobody Dale knew would voluntarily sleep face down in two feet of snow.

General Wellington glared at Dale in his mind. The Iron Duke was not forgiving.

"So," Dale said quietly. "Accident in back country. Park Rangers ride up to investigate. Rush right down into the middle of it without stopping to think."

Wilson's eyes kinda twinkled.

"Can you think of a better trap?" Dale asked.

Wilson smiled.

"Throw in a pretty girl needs rescuing," he observed.

Wilson hooked his reins on the saddle horn and drew his rifle.

"I'll cover," he said.

Dale thought about it, then rode Centurion down.

He could have left the brute up here, but that would have meant walking in both directions. Not good if he needed to run suddenly.

Hopefully, those damned Jayhawks wouldn't shoot a horse.

Down below, it was a mess.

The two horses whickered hopefully as he approached, still latched to their anchor and unable to move far.

The man was dead. Broken in unnatural directions. Turning blue.

Dale climbed down and drew his revolver. Centurion was trained enough to stay put.

No tracks other than Centurion's and the other two horses. That was good. Meant that nobody else was around, aiming at his back, and no scavengers had gotten the smell of death yet.

Those horses were pretty, too. A coal-black, matched pair of pretty ladies.

Friendly, too.

Dale pulled out one of the carrots he normally kept for Centurion and broke it in half, feeding pieces to the girls in spite of the utterly indignant snort coming from his own horse.

"Hello?" a voice whispered.

Dale was on his knees, tucked against the frame of the sleigh and aiming before his mind caught up. Even Centurion looked for someone to kick or stomp.

"Hello," the voice repeated. "Is someone there?"

It was coming from under the sleigh.

Dale looked closer at the box. Yard-high, metal gunwales all the way around, sloped for rough terrain like inverted shields. Sturdy, fiberglass ribs strung over the top holding up a heavy, white, canvas top that reminded Dale of a sail.

Crap kinda falling out all the gaps, from where everything inside had turned over and jumbled when the driver died.

Nobody was firing. Or charging.

And Wilson hadn't fired a warning shot through anyone, either.

"Here," Dale said back, just loud enough that someone close by could hear him.

"Oh, thank God," the exhausted voice replied.

Sounded like a woman.

Dale flashed back to Wilson's comment about pretty girls needing rescuing.

"Please help me," she said. "I'm trapped."

Dale took a long look in every direction, stood, and holstered his revolver.

He caught Wilson's eye and pointed at the sleigh.

The quiet giant nodded, seated up on that rise, still as dawn, sixty yards away, rifle covering the space.

Dale walked all the way around the wreckage.

Best way in looked to be the rear, so Dale pulled on the handle.

A box of something nearly crushed his foot before he hopped clear. It still blocked everything.

"Okay, that was dumb," he muttered to himself.

The sleigh was resting at an angle, tilted kinda like a lean-to, so Dale pulled out his Dad's old Buck knife and worked the steel edge into the canvas. It gave under the edge, once he forced it in, but it took all of Dale's weight to move it even two feet.

Good enough to look in.

Total mess.

Nothing had been tied down, but the top had held, so nothing had fallen out, either. And there had been a lot of junk in there. Mostly boxes, jumbled like puzzle pieces when you first open the box.

She was facing him from about five feet away.

Pretty.

Black hair all mussed. Dark eyes.

Lines cut deep into her cheeks from the pain.

Dale thrust the Buck knife in at an angle and sawed perpendicular, opening up a window big enough he could see.

Dale wasn't sure how she'd been sitting at that terrible moment, but the tumble had pinned her between two boxes, neither of which looked all that light.

"Help me, please," she whispered.

Dale nodded and stuck his shoulders inside. From here, he could see the hooks that held the white canvas taut. With a little weight, he was able to undo three of them and fold the cloth back.

It was slow but steady success.

He withdrew and pushed everything out of the way.

"Name's Dale, ma'am," he said as he worked.

"Cordelia," she replied.

Dale reached in and grabbed the nearest big box. It wiggled under his hands, and she screamed loud enough that Centurion kicked on general principle.

Dale fell on his ass letting go so suddenly.

"I am so sorry about that," Dale apologized as he got up.

Obviously, it was sitting *on* her leg.

Dale turned back to Wilson and shrugged big enough the man would hopefully understand. He certainly wasn't coming down here anytime soon.

Dale put one boot in and shifted around until he found a spot he could stand on ground and snow and not other boxes.

Now he was extra glad for all the weight-lifting machine work he did. Wilson's scrawny legs probably couldn't do *this*.

Dale squatted down and grabbed that box square. There was no space to twist, so he thrust straight upright before he turned and kinda shot-putted the box off the rear of the sleigh, out of the way. Damned thing weighed near a hundred pound, was his guess.

Her eyes were white, when he looked. All the blood had

drained out, but he didn't see any pools below her, and the leg wasn't bleeding. Wasn't exactly straight, either, but that was a problem for later.

She started to breathe again, a moment later. About the time Dale's breath slowed down enough to talk.

"Bad news, your leg is broken," he said, kinda serious. "Good news, you aren't a horse."

"Why is that good?" she asked, color slowly creeping back into her voice and her skin.

"Then I'd probably have to shoot you," Dale grinned. "I'm guessing that we'll just have to arrest you, instead."

"Why's that?" she said.

Rather than answer, Dale reached out and touched the nearest box, an old wooden chest with the saltire cross design of the Confederate States, the flyover successor to America, worked into the brass fittings.

Blue shirts.

Even a merchant crossing into the Colorado would know to remove something like that.

Fellow dead up front hadn't been expecting to be inspected. Hadn't hidden anything.

"Because you're a Jayhawk, ma'am," Dale said politely. "But first, I need to fix your leg."

"Oh."

Nothing else availing itself, Dale unbuttoned his overcoat and laid it oilskin-side-down in the snow outside the sleigh. There was no easy or soft way to do this, but it had to be done.

He moved close and kneeled beside her.

"Ma'am," he said quietly. "I'm going to pick you up and move you outside so I can splint your leg. It's going to hurt, but I have to do it. I'm sorry."

She nodded, gasping shallow and fast as he slid his right hand under her knee and put his left arm around her back. At least it was a mid-femur break. And hopefully clean, but they wouldn't know that until they x-rayed her at the hospital.

Dale was beginning to wonder if he'd be on a first-name basis with the Medevac crews, stuff like this kept up.

"Ready?" he asked.

She nodded, so he simply stood up.

She was a long girl, but willowy. Weighed next to nothing. Gritted her teeth but only whimpered in pain a time or two.

Dale pivoted slowly, careful not to bang her ends on anything as he turned.

A shadow suddenly blotted out the sunlight.

Centurion. Wondering what Dale was up to. Sticking his muzzle in to see if there were any treats.

"Move," Dale growled.

Horse might be dumb as a fence post, but he had enough empathy for a woman in pain. He backed out of the way.

Dale rested her on his overcoat and then climbed over the gunwale.

Centurion slobbered on his ear. Dale reached up and pushed the big head clear.

"You okay?" Dale asked.

She nodded.

He could tell she wasn't. Not really, but not willing to reveal too much.

He was still Johnny Law, today.

Dale looked up at Wilson and signaled with his hands that he had a medical situation, and that the coast looked clear. Wilson nodded and heeled Pronto into motion, but kept the rifle out.

You never knew.

"Be right back," Dale said.

He grabbed Centurion's reins and held him still long enough to retrieve the med kit.

She was wearing a skirt. Long even by Jayhawk standards, coming all the way to the tops of her lace-up boots. Only one layer of petticoat under it, from what he could tell, though.

"Ma'am, I'm going to need to lift your skirt so I can put something around your leg to immobilize it," Dale said. "Then I'm going to pull it and set the ends of the bone back together. Is it okay if I touch you to find the break?"

She looked at him puzzled. But it wasn't the confused-in-pain look. It was the nobody-ever-asked-first look. She nodded after a beat.

Dale rested on hand on her thigh, uncomfortably irregular, and the other on her knee.

It felt clean. With the chest off of it, it even looked straight. Dale pinched lightly until she hissed.

Yes, clean and aligned. He wouldn't even need to do more than put the brace on and inflate it. Let the docs back at barracks handle anything more complicated.

Dale blushed as he lifted her skirt and ran his hands over the skin of her thighs to set the brace. One little sound and it went rigid, holding the leg immobile.

Dale looked up as Pronto approached. The woman hissed, probably at the badge in the middle of Wilson's forehead.

Gold shield with a buffalo in the middle.

"Not as bad as I feared, sir," Dale said automatically.

Wilson nodded down at him. "Broken?"

"Yes, sir," Dale said.

Wilson laughed.

"Rescuing pretty girls, kid?"

Dale blushed so hard he thought the snow might melt, before he looked back over his shoulder at the wreck.

"Jayhawkers, Ranger," he said in a more formal tone.

The charming twinkle went out of those eyes.

She saw it, too. Flinched under Dale's hands.

Voice turned to ugly gravel

"Who's the driver?" Wilson demanded in a soft growl.

"Jameson Hunt," the woman said. Her voice changed, too. Angrier. "I supposed under Kansas law, he'd be considered my husband."

"Considered?" Wilson drawled.

Dale sat still and silent. He could still play good-cop if necessary.

"He bought me from a brothel in Dodge City," she said in a voice just this side of a challenging snarl. "Chattel might be as good a term."

"Smuggler?" Wilson challenged.

"Oh, probably," she replied in an exasperated tone. "Smooth talker. Gold miner. Big dreamer. Cut-throat card sharp. At least the son of a bitch is dead, now."

"You can still rot in that cell, instead, little lady," Wilson told her, his tones all flat and edged.

Dale felt a grin sneak in.

"A thought, Ranger," he interjected.

Wilson replied with an eyebrow. Dale turned to the woman, on an eye level with him.

She really was pretty, he could see that. And older than he had first guessed.

It was the eyes. Canny and hooded, but utterly exhausted when Dale looked close.

"You said he *bought* you from a brothel, did you not?" Dale asked, studying her like a rattlesnake he found on a sudden rock. The kind that might bite suddenly.

"That's right," she replied. "You'd be amazed what's legal in that territory."

Some of the angry had bled out of her voice. Misplaced, perhaps. Or reserved for that dead son of a bitch over there.

"Ah, no, lass," Wilson crooned in a voice utterly at odds with anything Dale had ever heard from or about the hard, quiet man. "I was born in Wichita. Little them folk do surprises me."

Dale blinked almost as hard as the woman did.

The moment of silent shock passed.

"So, Ranger," Dale continued. "Would this constitute a Mann Act violation?"

Wilson laughed outright. Once. Sharp. Mirthful.

"Kid, yer crazy," he said. "But I like the way you think."

"A what?" she asked, face screwed up sideways.

"Mann Act," Dale repeated. "Transporting a woman across state lines for immoral purposes. Yourself, perhaps."

"Why does it matter?" she snarled suddenly. "One more thing you can arrest me for? Throw me in jail for being debt-bonded, as well as a trespasser?"

"Nope," he grinned. "Just the opposite, as a matter of fact."

"What?"

Good, the confusion was back. She was prettier confused than angry.

Probably dangerous pretty, if she actually smiled.

Mom had always told him to trust the homely girls more. Pretty ones often got used to being able to get their way with just a smile. Homely ones had to actually work for something. Gave them more appreciation of other folk.

"Means you're the victim of one Jameson Hunt," Dale said. "Means we'll still confiscate most of this as contraband, maybe, but also means you'll probably be free to go. Or stay. Especially if there's a debt-bond for you on the other side of that state line."

Yup. Hard blink. Disbelieving.

Waiting for the other shoe to drop.

"What's the price?" she asked in a low, venomous tone.

Again, that never-been-asked-first tone.

"You'll have to put up with the two of us," Dale said. "And my doofus horse. At least until we can get you to barracks and processed. Superintendent will get involved at that point. Maybe even a Deputy Assistant Secretary, depending."

Dale looked up at Wilson.

"Or does this sort of thing fall under the purview of an Incident Commander?" he asked. "Statutes are kinda fuzzy on that topic."

"Kid, I don't read law books," Wilson answered.

Dale shrugged. Dad had always encouraged him to read. Mostly military theory and things he needed to become a Ranger, once Dale had set his mind to it, but also law, history, and philosophy, just to keep him well-rounded.

Nothing more boring than a man with only one topic he could discuss over the campfire.

The girl was looking at him now like he was the rattler.

Dale shrugged.

"Is this acceptable, Mrs. Hunt?" he asked.

More confusion.

Enlightenment.

"Draeger," she replied. "Cordelia Draeger. No way in hell I'm keeping his name."

Dale grinned at her.

"Miss Draeger," he agreed. "Let's get you home."

Dale laughed every time Centurion snorted in angry disgust, trailing behind the sleigh as it carved through the snow. It had taken very little work to convince the two carriage horses to help him pull the sleigh back upright. Little more to fix up their harness so they could pull it, with a mightily disgusted Centurion running along behind..

He and Wilson had arranged the crap in back well enough for a bed, but Cordelia had insisted on riding up front on the bench with him, right leg splayed out funny, like a wishbone, under the blanket, while Wilson rode escort.

And she had refused anything more than a couple of pain tablets.

Tough woman.

Or maybe she still didn't trust them not to slip her a mickey. He could guess how other men had treated her along the way from the pain he saw occasionally in her eyes.

Jameson Hunt got wrapped up in a blanket and stowed, frozen solid after a day dead in the snow. He wouldn't melt before they got back, cutting straight again instead of finishing the patrol.

And now, two ladies in black coats pulling. Bobbed tails with bells in them, presumably to warn off bears and critters.

And one indignant Centurion tied to the rear and being pulled bodily along, any time he slowed down or sped up.

Wilson had ridden ahead, the last few miles, so as to round up a vet and a doc. Both were waiting at the open gate, along with Wilson, Stan Hawkins, and a slew of others as Dale and Cordelia approached in the sleigh.

"So what happens to me now?" she asked.

"Not up to me," Dale replied. "But you've got a good story if you stick with it."

"But everything will be confiscated," she said.

"Maybe," Dale agreed. "And maybe only his things. Not like we'd debt-bond you again, five minutes after we rescued you."

"He had money," Cordelia whispered over the thump of hooves and the hiss of snow. "Hidden in a chest."

"Ma'am, greenbacks are worthless in Colorado," he said. "Did he have any gold? Or Loonies?"

"No."

She fell silent, dejected.

"However," Dale began with a grin. "If you didn't need to return to Kansas, you could probably sell those two lovely horses to the Service for a goodly stake. Maybe some of the other gear as well. Enough to live on while you figured out what you were wanting to do with this freedom."

The way she turned suddenly and studied his face made Dale blush. Harder than usual. He'd never met too many pretty women.

"How old are you Dale?" she asked. "And just what is your last name?"

"Embry, ma'am," he replied. "Sixteen. Be seventeen in the spring."

"I'm too old for you, Dale Embry," she said, deadly serious, causing his blush to double. "And that's a shame. But I'll listen to your advice."

Dale let the silence and the snow engulf them at that point.

He had a pretty good idea what she was implying. It left him uncomfortable.

At least there was a crowd gathered in the square by the time he got the sleigh halted.

Stan walked over, arm still done up in a sling. Wilson was next to him, and Pronto had to say hi to the ladies pulling. The doc and the vet were there, too.

"I'm taking the kid fly-fishing with me, next summer," Wilson announced to Stan.

The old man just kinda stared at the Ranger as Dale sat

there. There was too much crowd for him to get out and help, and nothing being left undone, with so many folks around.

"Hey," Wilson continued. "We went out looking for bad guys, and look what he brought home. Imagine what it would be like if we were after trout."

That got a laugh and a cheer from the crowd that made Dale want to curl up and die of embarrassment, right here.

Cordelia didn't help.

She leaned over and grabbed him. Pulled him close.

Kissed him full on the lips and held on as he squirmed. Warmed his whole soul up, though.

If anything, the cheering got louder.

FORTY-NINER

February wasn't starting much better than January had, but at least they'd gone a whole week without more snow.

Dale loved living in the Laramie Mountains of northern Colorado, and patrolling in the Roosevelt Forest, but he was about wintered out at this point. At least he had four whole days to himself, starting right about now.

Better, Stan was just about ready to be medically certified for duty again. Wilson had been a pleasant boss to work for, but he wasn't nearly as broadly read as Stan Hawkins, the Last Ranger, was. Campfire was kinda boring with Wilson, not that Dale would ever say that out loud.

And today, Dale could have even slept clear until the sun came up, but he hadn't done that in years, even in summer. Life in the Service, protecting the Rockies from the Huskers and Jayhawks of the Confederate States. The place his Dad still called flyover country.

No, up at four AM, all set to build up the fire for tea and a hot breakfast, even though he didn't have to.

Today, somebody else got to cook.

From the looks of things, he was about third to breakfast this morning, beating even the Rangers and Guides who were going to be headed out in a bit. The biscuits were still steaming fresh, so he grabbed three and cut them open on his plate, adding sausage patties, scrambled eggs, diced potatoes, and some shredded cheese to the pile, before pouring a ladleful of chewy, cream gravy over top of the mess.

He found an empty table, set his plate and a glass of orange juice down, and went back to steep some tea. Good stuff, too. Transported from California, with summer honey brought in from Aspen.

Someone was seated across from his food when Dale turned around and headed back. There was a whole, empty mess hall to pick from, so maybe they just wanted some company.

The crutches resting against the wall made him do a double-take, but he recognized her, even dressed up way differently than he was used to. And she cleaned up amazing well.

Cordelia Draeger.

Ex-Jayhawk. Former debt-bonded prostitute.

Former lot of things, most of which she hadn't actually said aloud, but were there in her eyes.

She had kept her black hair medium length and tied back, but wore almost no makeup these days. This morning, the woman was wearing a gray sweatshirt with the Colorado School of Mines on the front. A leftover handed down, because she had almost no clothes of her own. Cordelia had told him that she was never again wearing clothes *that man*, Jameson Hunt, had bought for her.

Clothes *he* had bought when he had bought her from a brothel in Dodge City.

All she ended up keeping were the pretty, lace-up boots with the narrow heel. The rest was Park Service gear. The green pants everybody wore. Simple black t-shirts, since she wasn't in the Service, but just staying on here until she healed.

And figured out what she wanted to do with the rest of her life.

Hopefully, her motives were pure, today. She was probably the prettiest girl Dale had ever met, but he was sixteen and she was thirty-two. And way more worldly.

And far less educated.

He tried to treat her like a big sister. So did most of the camp, near as he could tell.

"Morning, Cordelia," he said, all proper and relaxed-like as he sat down and grabbed a spoon to start shoveling.

She had maybe one scrambled egg worth on her plate, and one biscuit. With a single, lonely sausage link on the side.

To Dale, that looked like the snack he ate while waiting in line for dinner.

"Dale," she said, eyes all a-twinkle at him.

Standing, she was near his height, but it was all leg. Seated, she was nearly a head shorter. He felt like a giant today.

Dale figured silence would be a good weapon now. Almost as good as a mouth full of food, when he was in need of a moment to think. He shoveled the first messy bite home.

He would've guessed she had younger brothers, from the way her eyes sorta rolled at him and she shook her head, never losing her grin as she watched him eat.

"Thank you, again," she said.

It was a regular occurrence. They could have thrown her in jail as a trespasser.

Instead, being a rescued sexual-trafficking victim meant she got to claim all of Jameson Hunt's goods. Him being dead of accidental causes before they arrived had helped.

Selling it all off, along with those two, lovely, coal-black carriage horses, had set her up well enough that she could probably go years without needing a job, if she exercised care.

Dale nodded. And shoveled.

Safe. Both ways.

"I came across something in one of the boxes that I kept," she continued, her voice suddenly dropping to the point where Dale's own chewing was almost too loud.

Dale swallowed and leaned forward. Not much. Enough.

"I told you that bastard was a card sharp and a gold miner," she said, referring the late, unlamented Jameson Hunt. "He had a treasure map."

Dale snorted and shoveled another bite of heaven home.

"What?" she pleaded.

Dale sucked down some tea to clear his mouth. Which was a dumb idea, since it was still too hot. He managed to not spray her with any as he coughed.

When he finally got settled, Dale smiled at her.

"There's no gold around here that anybody's missed, Cordelia," he said, pointing at her sweatshirt. "Miners have been at it for a long time, looking."

"Well it's marked, and he paid some fellow good money for it, down in Guymon, Oklahoma," she retorted.

Something about her face changed, all of a sudden.

Closed up.

Blink, and she turned into somebody entirely else. Just like that.

If he hadn't been watching so close, he would have missed it.

The only clue was the way her eyes had flitted over his right shoulder, just for the faintest moment.

Dale glanced back.

Stan had come in and was standing there with his breakfast in hand. Not close enough to be rude or hear anything, but obvious.

"May I join you?" Stan asked, pointedly looking at Cordelia.

Dale glanced over, saw how taut she had wound herself.

"It's okay," he said. "Stan's one of the good guys."

She nodded. Tight. Precise.

Like she didn't trust words right now.

Dale pushed his chair back and rose.

"Cordelia Draeger," he said. "May I introduce Stan Hakwins? The Last Ranger."

"The Last?" she asked suddenly in a confused tone. Back to where she was before, maybe.

Stan took the chair next to Dale and put his food and tea down.

"I was the last Ranger authorized under the old United States of America, Miss Draeger," he said. "Thirty-five years ago, before the Park Service went rogue. Before things went to hell and the country where I was born turned into several smaller ones that didn't particularly like each other."

Dale watched her blink again, and maybe unwind a trifle. Less like a spooked horse, anyway.

"Hawkins?" Cordelia asked, after a breath.

Stan nodded, just sipping his morning tea.

"You were there after Dale and Wilson rescued me."

"That's right," Stan agreed. "Wilson's been covering my territory while my shoulder healed."

"What happened?" she asked.

"Got shot by a group of trespassing Jayhawkers," Stan replied, eyes all a-glitter with inner laughter.

"I'm sorry," she said, face falling.

"Its fine, now," Stan said. "Kid dropped a mountain on them. Taught 'em proper manners."

The look Cordelia gave him made Dale blush all over again.

All he had done was trigger the explosives Stan had set. After Stan ordered him to, with Stan sprawled right in the middle of the blast zone.

Hold my beer, indeed.

Cordelia studied Dale close as he went back to eating. And blushing some more.

Finally, she decided.

"I was telling Dale about something I found in Jameson Hunt's personal papers," she said, not much above a whisper, even as the three of them were alone in a corner. "A map to a hidden gold mine."

Stan glanced over at Dale, so he shrugged.

"Gold mine," Stan observed laconically. Not quite disbelief in those tones. "Forty-niner?"

It was two centuries ago, and three states away, when Forty-niner referred to the folks who had gone to California, in 1849, looking for gold. The term had stuck, even today.

"And Dale said that was impossible," she continued.

Stan quick nodded at him this time. Respectful. Appreciative, Dale hoped.

"Would you be willing to share it with us?" Dale asked.

Again, she had that blink of surprise that evaporated quickly.

This woman just wasn't used to being asked politely. For anything.

It didn't help Dale's opinion of Jayhawks and Huskers, but they had chosen the kind of country they wanted. One where the opinions of women weren't much listened to.

Morons.

She took a deep breath, held it, and then nodded after a moment..

Lifted up her sweatshirt enough to pull out a paper map sealed in a plastic map sleeve that had been tucked into her waistband. Where nobody might steal it while she was at breakfast.

A thought struck Dale.

"How much did he pay for this map?" Dale asked.

Cordelia's eyes got narrow. Pained.

Angry.

"More than he did for me," she finally hissed.

Dale had a hankering to go piss on Jameson Hunt's grave. It was probably a fairly widely held opinion, as Miss Draeger charmed the men and women of the barracks. He might have to get in line to do it.

Stan had taken the sleeve from her hand and spread the map out flat between them, food all moved to the side for the moment and forgotten. Mostly forgotten. Dale didn't want the gravy getting cold, so he shoveled smaller bites and listened.

Stan Hawkins was The Last Ranger for a reason.

"Rough, nasty country in the North Laramie Mountains," he observed, touching two spots on either side of the red mark. "Closer to Diamond Peak than Iron Mountain. Not many people up there ever. Pretty much none, today."

He paused, ruminating on something.

"Dale, I know you had some time off scheduled," he began.

"Ranger, I am still only a Guide, and subject to your orders," Dale interjected with a grin.

It was an old game.

Stan had told the Superintendent and others that he thought Dale should be promoted. Bureaucrats didn't like upset apple carts. The Rangers listened to Stan more than the Superintendent, though.

"Well in that case, *young man*," Stan grinned back. "I'll just ask Wilson to stay on a couple of days, and you and I will go have an adventure."

He fixed Cordelia with a steely eye.

"You are aware, Miss Draeger," he continued with a serious mien, "that the Service pays a finder's fee for things like this?"

She blinked again. Like today was a vastly more educational experience than she had expected, getting up so early.

"Thought not," Stan said with a grin. "There will be more paperwork when we get back, but for now, I'll let the Incident Commander know what we're up to, and maybe the Deputy Secretary."

Dale was still amazed at the thought that Stan, his friend and mentor, could just ring up the Deputy Secretary of the Interior to chat.

"Enjoy your breakfast, you two," Stan said, picking up his plate, cup, and the map. "We'll probably head out around sunrise.

Cordelia looked like she was in shock again, so Dale shoveled quickly. He'd be back to making breakfast tomorrow.

Might as well enjoy one last, good meal.

***

Dale had brought extra carrots for Centurion. The big blue roan would never admit to jealousy, but Dale knew his horse. The beast hadn't forgotten Dale pulling him along behind Cordelia's sleigh, letting the two black beauties get the glory. At least the grooms had already gotten him saddled and ready when he and Stan arrived.

Audrey stood there like a queen, but she was the Last Ranger's horse. Her spot in the pecking order was set, and she knew it.

Gear and preparation took another thirty minutes. Best to do it all right and careful.

As they rode up to the front gate, the Ranger of the Guard smiled at them and checked her clipboard.

"Hawkins and Embry, headed out," she called, saluting.

They saluted back, and Dale hoped the Superintendent was dead fast asleep. Only Rangers warranted the Call. She should have said "Ranger Hawkins, headed out."

One of these days, that was likely to get him in trouble, but there was nothing he could do about it until the Superintendent decided he was ready to be promoted from Guide to Ranger.

Because they were the proud descendent of the old National Park Service, before it went rogue, just before the second American Revolution, he and Stan rode horses. There were trucks. And all manner of aircraft on call. It might have taken all of twenty minutes to drop on the spot from above.

But Stan was old school. Forty miles as the crow flies. Maybe sixty or seventy on roads and trails. A good day's hard ride to keep the horses in shape.

And you saw a lot more of the terrain on horseback than you ever would, flying over it, or romping along in a four-wheel-drive vehicle. Far harder to hide from the Rangers.

The day passed quickly. Conversations on law, history, and trail lore. Again, far more interesting than the almost-silent Wilson.

The Service might have thought that Dale needed seasoning before he was ready for the hat and the badge, but he was getting the best education possible along the way. Stan Hawkins had never moved beyond Ranger because everybody else had to spend too much time indoors, doing paperwork.

Or worse, back in Sacramento doing politics.

Dale shuddered with an emotion he couldn't describe. Not fear. Not disgust.

Disdain, perhaps, for cutting yourself off from all this beauty.

Even putting up with a big, loveable goof like Centurion, as like to chase a rabbit as to spook at one. Audrey was never that silly.

Dale knew better than to be concerned that Stan hadn't looked at the map once after they left Rustic Barracks. There weren't that many ways to get where they were going. Up Old 69 and over to the Red Feather Lakes area, where they got a nice burger at a trading post gas station, and then loop up clockwise into the wilderness.

Nightfall found them in a little copse of trees with a tarp slung to break up any wind and weather, a nice fire, and a tent tucked in close. Dinner was tea and flatcakes, with some meat they had brought along, the cold keeping it frozen most of the day.

Morning found them on the move, already past Iron Mountain and headed roughly north.

Stan finally dug the map out about thirty minutes after the sun came up in a sky so blue, so bright, so cold as to be painful.

He turned Audrey to the left and studied the hillside. Dale waited, silent and patient.

Finally Stan turned to him.

"The old eyes just aren't what they used to be, Dale," he said. "Find me a discontinuity on that slope."

Dale wasn't sure what he meant, but pulled his binoculars out and began to quarter the hillside slowly.

He must have stopped too long, or forgotten to breathe.

"What have you found?" Stan asked.

Dale couldn't describe it. Wouldn't have seen it, but for Stan using the word *discontinuity*. White from snow. Green from trees.

And *something*.

"No," Stan said. "It wouldn't be obvious. Where?"

"Twenty degrees right of center," Dale tried to point. "About two thirds up. Is that our gold mine?"

"Might be," Stan said. "In the right place. Let's ride."

Dale was technically the Guide here, an *090*, but he knew better than to suggest he knew trailcraft better than Stan. Might not be anybody that knew the Colorado winter better than Stan Hawkins did. Dale followed the man up the hill happily.

They were on the lee side here, with a lot of trees, so the snow wasn't that deep. Twenty minutes saw them to the place where *something* hadn't looked right.

As they came around a corner and over a rise, it became obvious they were in the right place, whatever that meant. It took Dale a moment to identify, then it was obvious.

The discontinuity was a square area where nature never intended one, but one that you would miss unless you were looking. There was even a trail of sorts up to it, or the remains of one. Enough for critters to use. They had.

And it had survived through however long. Once Centurion stomped his big feet on it, Dale understood why. Someone had poured a full concrete driveway up here, slightly sloped, and then left it for decades to accumulate pine needles and dirt.

Dale looked closer.

Someone had also built a wall with that concrete, but left it rough and then painted it in a camouflage pattern of evergreen and dirt.

At the top of the clearing stood a forty-foot-wide wall with a ten-foot-wide garage door in the middle and a slightly recessed human-scale door to the right side.

Stan pulled Audrey's reins and dismounted, a step ahead of Dale. Both horses got loose-tied to nearby trees, so they could graze and wait.

"Any ideas?" Dale asked.

"According to our map, this is the gold mine, Dale," Stan said with a little awe. "Never even heard about something like this, in thirty years of being a Ranger around here."

"Rifles?" Dale inquired, reaching out to touch the holster on Centurion's saddle.

"Nope," Stan replied. "In close quarters, you want a pistol in hand. Easy to maneuver if something jumps out. Heavy enough to use as a hammer or a club. Rifle just gets in the way."

Huh. Good to know.

"What should we bring?" Dale asked, looking over the gear that the two horses carried.

"Flashlights, medkit, and a crowbar," Stan replied. "Anything else, we'll come back for it."

Dale grabbed what they needed, stuffed it into pockets, and followed Stan to the door.

Steel. Painted over with something tough. Kinda reminded him of marine paint, only green. Nothing at all growing on it, just a layer of splashed grime from countless winters. Hinges on the outside, turning on pins thicker than his thumb.

Instead of a traditional handle, there was a wheel of sorts. A really small version of the old ship's wheel from pirate movies, only barely eighteen inches across.

"You're young and strong," Stan said. "Have a go at turning this. Counter-clockwise."

Dale nodded and rested everything to one side. He stopped, and ran back to Centurion for some machine lubricant. The good stuff. Made the world go.

Couple of spritzes and some gunk oozed out of the bottom.

"Good thinking," Stan observed.

Dale left his gloves on and grabbed hold of two of the bars sticking out, just like a pirate captain. He squatted underneath the thing and drove himself upwards. Like Wilson, Stan's legs were bowed and kinda scrawny. Most Rangers didn't work the machines to stay in shape with the dedication Dale did.

Wheel sounded like death clawing its way out of the grave, from one of the old movies, but it moved. Dale jerked it back down when it stopped moving. Dad had taught him about torque on old steel. Sure enough, it passed the old resting point and twisted another five or ten degrees.

Dale thought about it and sprayed some more lubricant into the gap.

He put his shoulder into the wheel. It moved a bit and then stopped. Dale grunted and breathed out.

This time, something broke. The wheel suddenly turned freely in his hands, still screaming in pain, but mobile.

Dale gave it two full rotations and then it stopped moving with a clunk. The kind of sound where it said, "I'm done."

Dale continued to suck air, and pulled on the wheel. It didn't want to come, so Dale put a foot up on the frame and put all his weight behind it.

Something popped and the door swung free, nearly dumping him on his ass before he got his balance back.

Stan stepped past him, revolver drawn and held firm, hammer down, but thumb up on it for a quite snap-shot. He'd been doing this for a long time.

Dale unbuttoned his overcoat a little, enough to breathe, and picked everything up. Medkit was safe in a pocket, but he still had a crowbar and a flashlight.

He figured Stan could shoot anything that needed killing, but he could still hit them with the bar.

Through the vault door, Dale found Stan examining a second door. There was light in here, diffuse, but enough. The roof was made of some sort of quartz set into the concrete slope. Sufficient to keep things lit. The space felt like a garage, but it was empty as a tomb. You could have fit a pair of trucks in the space, easy.

"Good news, nobody's ever found this place," Stan said.

"Bad news?" Dale asked.

"Door's still locked," Stan pointed.

There was a padlock on a hasp. You could turn the handle, but the door wouldn't move. And the whole frame in here was concrete as well.

"Fortunately, we've got a crowbar," Stan said. "Otherwise, we'd have to try shooting it off and hope the ricochet didn't kill anyone."

Scary idea.

Dale looked at the setup. He could get underneath, and slip the chisel end in.

Yup, just barely fit, but it was in.

He got below it and held the bar overhead, standing slowly and putting all his strength into it. Stan was wiry. Wilson was kinda soft in the middle. Most of the Rangers he knew didn't have the physical strength to do this.

He might have to mention that to an Incident Commander, when they got home. Quietly, though. Dale had a pretty good idea how people would take the suggestion for more exercise.

Archimedes would have been proud, though.

Three feet of steel generated enough torque that he could feel the lock's innards bowing in pain, before they finally surrendered with a gunshot sound. Dale pushed opened the door and pulled the flashlight from his pocket.

Inside was dim, but not black. Again, overhead quartz. Someone had designed this place well. And the inside of the door had a spot for a nearby steel bar to be braced against it.

Dale started to move forward, but Stan caught his arm.

"Let it breathe," he said.

Breathe?

"Place like that's been closed up for a long time," Stan continued. "Air goes bad, especially if it's a mine."

Dale nodded and waited. The air inside was blowing softly out, warmer than the outside air, so Dale figured they had a good chimney effect going. Dryer, too, which was probably a good sign.

After a few minutes, Stan nodded and flipped on his flashlight, the cold, white beam cutting the dimness inside to show a second room that was also raw concrete. It felt like a mud room.

Sure enough, a pair of badly-aged, square-toe boots sat to one side. Farmer style, rather than the cowboy boots Dale and Stan had on. Hooks set into the wall held a couple of old jackets.

Dale followed Stan in.

The inner space was a room about ten feet square, walls and floors square with more concrete, painted a soft blue. There was nothing on the walls, only a few throw rugs on the floor, and an open doorway on the left going further back. No dust and no moisture, so it had been sealed well, whenever that had been.

Stan touched a light switch and flipped it, but nothing happened. He shrugged.

"Worth a try," he said. "There was power here at one point."

Stan went through the doorway with Dale in his wake.

"Feels like a house, and not a mine," Dale ventured.

"I agree," Stan said.

They were in a hallway now, more quartz bricks in the ceiling giving enough light to see. Dale knew he'd have to climb up there at some point, just to see how the architect had done it. He didn't figure Stan would know what a Hobbit house was, but they were inside one now.

Down the hall was a doorway. No door, just a cast concrete frame. Stan stuck his flashlight around the corner as he approached, revolver held back close to the body.

Dale gripped the crowbar and considered an overhead strike. He'd never played ball growing up, happier to spend his summers in the mountain meadows, but he knew how to hit a baseball. Just never cared to do it.

"Well what do we have here?" Stan said, entering the room with a firm step.

Dale followed, and found himself facing an antique

electrical generator on a rolling frame. Machine oil scent permeated the stone.

It had been a long time coming, but the three plastic jugs sitting next to the beast were empty when Dale touched them. Either they had been left thus, or long forgotten.

Next to them was a pressurized water tank, also empty when Stan tapped on the side, as well as a big cistern tank that did drip when Dale turned the stopcock.

"Why two?" Dale asked

"There's a well," Stan replied. "The other is draining from the hillside somewhere."

"No gunk?" Dale sniffed.

"Silver in the tank, plus skylights for sunlight, that ought to be sufficient."

"Gold mine?" Dale finally asked the important question.

"Somewhere below," Stan answered.

They went back into the hallway. To the end.

Stairs down. Light revealed painted walls and a big throw rug on the level below. Dale followed the Last Ranger down.

Living room. Big, wood-framed sofa. Comfy chair that just screamed dry-rot. Side tables. Landscapes on the walls.

And bookshelves everywhere.

Hardcovers. Paperbacks. Trades.

History. Politics. Law. Biographies. Thrillers. Mysteries. Science Fiction. Romance. Historic. More.

Abandoned, but not dusty. Just forgotten. Like the owner went out for supplies one day and never came back. Dale had to tear himself away before he touched all of them.

He wanted to steal them all. Centurion would never go for the weight.

Back half of the level was a kitchen. Pantry with cans and jars so old Dale had never heard of most of the brands. Cold box set into the wall. You might have butter, but milk would have been a pain, unless you went to the store weekly.

This place didn't feel like the man who owned it went out much. And it was a man who decorated. Everything was dark, earth tones and wood. Masculine, like Dad's den, back home in Hood River, Oregon.

One more staircase down and they found a bedroom that took up the whole floor. Maybe bedroom was the wrong word. Library, with a small daybed tucked into one corner. Single wide, so the man was alone. Desk in another corner. Every other surface was covered with handmade bookcases, stuffed to the gills with thousands of books, including the side of the staircase up and another one, going down.

"What's that?" Dale asked, pointing to a rusted, metal *something* on the desk.

"That, my young friend, is a mechanical typewriter," Stan observed with a smile in his voice. "Probably at least a century old. Back before the electronic versions that were already gone when I was a kid, even before the computers that replaced them."

Stan grinned at him.

"And I know you want to touch all the books, but let's go to the bottom of our mine first," Stan continued. "It's been all concrete so far, so I'm not worried about rot. Good concrete like this takes a century to even set, and five more before it decides to rot."

Dale nodded. Old, medieval towers had been built to last forever. So had this place.

He wondered anew about the man who had just never come home one day.

One more floor and they found his workshop. Powertools. A drill press. Lathe. Table saw. Chop saw. Other thing Dale couldn't identify.

Shelves and cabinets filled with mechanical and hand tools. Planes. Hand drill. Saws of every size and description. Everything.

Dale drooled almost as hard here as he had at all the books.

But this was it. There was a sump pump in one corner, but no more stairs. And some of these walls were actual stone, carved with tools and blasted with dynamite, from the bore holes he found.

But nothing else. Nothing deeper.

No gold mine.

They brought the horses into the garage and set up camp there, secure from the weather and reasonably comfortable when they pulled some downed limbs in to provide beds.

Nightfall came early in the winter.

Dale was holding a biography of the Ben Franklin he had never even heard of before. Not reading it, so much as wondering at it.

"So what happened?" he finally asked Stan.

The Last Ranger shrugged and sipped his tea.

"Who knows, Dale?" he replied. "He went out for supplies and something happened to stop him from coming home. Maybe he went home to die and told someone about this place. They drew a map, and it became a thing."

"But, why call it a gold mine?"

Dale was puzzled.

Stan grinned.

"I think we have a game of telephone, my boy," the Ranger said.

"Telephone?"

Now Dale was twice as puzzled. They didn't have telephones in the deep country. Too hard to get a signal, unless you broadcast a signal of your own. That just let bad people find you.

Or avoid you.

It was one of the reasons Rangers and Guides had to train so hard. You were out there on your own, with only an emergency radio to call for help. And even then, the cavalry might be hours from saving your butt, depending.

"From before even my time, Dale," Stan sighed. "It goes like this. I call you up and tell you something. You call up a friend and tell them. Then they tell someone else. And so it goes. Things're bound to get garbled along the way."

"But, a gold mine? I still don't get it."

"So I have all these books," Stan continued. "And the tools. And the world is coming apart. You're too young to remember the days we thought a nuclear war was coming, but Armageddon seemed imminent. Especially after that idiot President nuked Los Angeles. Those books and tools would be of immeasurable value if something happened."

Dale nodded, still not convinced.

"So he told someone he had a treasure hidden out there in the mountains," Stan tried again. "And he was in Kansas, or Oklahoma. Somewhere over the line where nobody could get to it. Draws a map. Sells it. The second fellow sells it on to a third, and mentions treasure, but not what that treasure is. Years pass. Fourth fellow sells it, but he thinks treasure means gold, so this must be a mine."

"Telephone," Dale finally understood. "Jameson Hunt buys the map, thinking it is literally a mine, so he brought some of the supplies we saw, thinking he would get rich with gold. Forty-niner."

"Exactly," Stan smiled.

"So now what?" Dale asked.

"The Service will claim the place and pay Miss Draeger a reward," Stan said. "With a little work, this would be a nice, comfy place for a sub-station or a watch tower. Most of the books will go to a library somewhere. Same with the tools. After China died, nobody was making those tools, or buying them. And a lot of that stuff down there was made in the old America, a century or more ago."

"But why do it in the first place?" Dale asked. "Why build a place like this in the middle of nowhere, and then abandon it?"

Stan studied him for a moment, before his eyes filled with understanding.

"Some days, I forget you're only sixteen, Dale," the Last Ranger said with a heavy voice. "Maybe he wanted to be alone in the mountains. But we all grow old. Things like this outlive us all, but we have to not let anything be forgotten." •

Stan paused to stare at some invisible horizon for a few moments before he continued.

"The Confederate States don't want much of that fancy book-learning. Fear it taints folks to know too much. Coastal

Republic feels different. Educates women. Makes them be politicians, even."

"There's so much we've lost, Stan," Dale finally whispered.

"More than I care to think about, young man," Stan said. "Some of those books might be the only copies in existence. A priceless treasure, to the right folks."

"So Jameson Hunt really was a gold miner, a Forty-Niner, after all?" Dale asked.

"I suppose so," Stan said. "But so are you, Dale. However, you'll get far more value from this mine than that man could have. It is all about perception."

Dale looked down at Ben Franklin's face again.

Forty-niners.

Both he and Jameson Hunt had gone looking for a gold mine. But he would have succeeded, where Jameson Hunt would have considered it a failure. Dale had no doubt that the man who would buy a wife from a brothel wouldn't be about to share all this significance. From what he'd heard about the man, Jameson Hunt would have never even seen the value in his gold mine. Just disgust that it was all books and worthless tools when he'd been hoping to get rich.

Dale knew he would claim a few books as his, and Stan would look the other way, because there were truck-loads down there that could go to a library in Fort Collins. Or Denver. Or even Sacramento, if they were rare enough to be added the Library of the Republic.

You just had to find the gold in your own life. And he had.

That probably did make him a Forty-Niner.

POSSE

D ale watched the man in the bright green uniform with so many gold bangles make the same mistake so many others had, standing at the front of the small, packed auditorium in front of a whiteboard hastily erased in case he had wanted to write something.

The Army General had asked if there were any questions.

Dale wanted to say nothing. Do nothing. Let the moment pass.

He couldn't help himself, even as the youngest person in the room, still a few weeks shy of his seventeenth birthday. The rest were all grown-ups by comparison, Rangers and other Guides, frequently with decades on him.

Still, Dad hadn't raised him to shirk his duties. His hand went up.

The Peacock pointed at him.

"Young man?" he asked, in a voice that really wanted to be deep and authoritative, but came out nasally and kinda annoying. Like the rest of the General.

"Why?" Dale asked.

It sounded rude, even in his own ears.

"Why what?" the general fired back, anger growing evident at being challenged by a teenager.

Dale suspected the man had shoes older than Dale was. He chewed on the words, trying to find a less insulting way to phrase his question.

Stan Hawkins, the Last Ranger, rescued him.

"I believe what Mr. Embry is trying to say, and Dale, please correct me," Stan said, his own voice pitched to call cattle in an open field. "Why is this battle, this war, even necessary?"

Stan glanced at him for confirmation.

Dale blushed, but nodded. Far less rude than probably would have come out of his mouth. Stan probably knew that.

"What on Earth are you talking about, Ranger?" the General growled.

Here was an adult the General could tussle with. Maybe even one he knew and had a *history* with. Everyone knew Stan Hawkins.

"The state line is good enough for both sides," Dale finally said, unwilling to make Stan fight this battle for him. "Has been for a long time. Both sides respect it, most of the time. If we attack them, what do we gain? Territory we can't hold? A civilian population that resents us? Where is the benefit commensurate with the effort?"

In his mind, Dale watched the Duke of Wellington put his arm around William Tecumseh Sherman's shoulders, both men grinning ear to ear and laughing approvingly.

"This is a war, Embry," the General snarled. "We do not question policy."

"With all due respect, General, the Park Service is not part of your chain of command." Dale fired back, feeling something catch fire in his belly. "*18 USC 1385*. Posse Comitatus. We're the civilian law enforcement here, and it cuts both ways. We answer to the Secretary of the Interior, not the Secretary of War. All this attack of yours will do is stir people up. If it's a raid, like those Jayhawkers did to us over the winter, that's one thing. What the hell do you gain from occupying Hays, Kansas? Except to throw up an awful lot of refugees and folks in the worst part of what the almanac says will be a miserable, wet spring. It sounds an awful lot like you expect us to take care of them for you. And we will, but there are better ways to handle our job."

"You are a Guide, Embry," the General said in a cold, vicious voice. "You will do what we tell you. Is that clear?"

Stan Hawkins was known in the Service as the Last Ranger He was the last man authorized as a United States Park Ranger under the old United States government, thirty-five years ago. Before the rebellions that broke the nation into a handful of smaller countries. And after what would become the Confederate States dropped a nuclear bomb on downtown Los Angeles.

Stan was a tall man, perhaps an inch above Dale's six foot one. Skinnier, though, weighing maybe one hundred seventy pounds to Dale's one ninety-five. Fifty-eight years old to Dale's almost-seventeen.

Mean as a hungry snake, when pushed.

Like now.

Stan stood up slowly as the room turned deadly silent. Stared at the general for a long, terrible moment.

A man cast in white bronze.

"What Embry says goes for me, as well, General," he said in a voice reminiscent of doom as he gestured at the folks around him. "And, I suspect, a great many of the men and women in this room. You'll answer him, and us, or you can leave. But you will speak to us all with respect while you remain. Am I clear?"

For a moment, Dale wondered if seconds would be needed in the coming duel. As well as how many people, himself included, would volunteer without hesitation, if Stan asked.

Something of that must have been obvious to the General. He glowered at Stan, then Dale, and then the entire room. Staring daggers. After a moment, he stomped out, slamming a door open and then closed.

Silence was like snowfall.

Dale figured he'd stepped in it, but good, this time.

Someone was going to make calls. This was probably going to go all the way to the top, back in Sacramento, just as fast as that man's angry fingers could dial numbers. Under Secretaries talking to one another and proffering position papers and memos replete with bureaucratic jargon. Secretary of War yelling profanities at the Secretary of the Interior. He was known to be like that.

Dale wondered what he would do for a living once they kicked him out of the Park Service.

Stan turned to him in the utter silence as the other Ranger and Guides watched.

"Dale, I don't think I've said this enough," Stan announced with utter conviction. "You make me proud to be a Ranger, and I consider it an honor to call you a friend."

The room erupted. Cheers, when Dale was expecting abuse and insults.

Others suddenly crowded around to pat him on the shoulder or back or head.

Dale blushed, and kept his own counsel.

The field side of the service, *090*'s and *025*'s, Guides and Rangers, were on his side. He knew that. There was still all the administrative folks to deal with. And the Superintendent of Rustic Barracks really didn't like him all that much.

***

Dale was way too young to be drinking, even if everyone else in the room wasn't. He settled for a mug of decaffeinated tea cut with vanilla and honeyed cream while Stan drank a small glass of brandy and Wilson sipped at a very dry Syrah imported at great expense from Australia of all places, itself broken into pieces by the wars of the last generation.

Dale kept waiting for the other shoe to drop. Guides didn't sass Generals. Even stupid ones.

For now, though, the bar was a happy place. Stan had infected everyone with his bravado. Morale was extremely high. There repercussions could wait for tomorrow. Or could have.

Superintendent Azad entering the room smothered all the energy, noise stuttering down to nothing as the man appeared. All eyes followed him. Even the piano player stopped in the middle of his tune.

Azad stopped a few steps inside the door to the bar, glancing right and left, aware that he had everyone's attention. Reveling in it.

Hilar Azad was a small man. Five foot six. Late-forties. Thin and weedy, but with a deep, solid voice, and a sharp mind. He had come up from the *303* side, the clerks and bureaucrats who kept the Service running, day in and day out. He commanded Rustic Barracks with a firm hand, but an honest one. A man who was well respected, if not always liked.

Azad walked up to the table Dale shared with the two older Rangers. Eyed them each before settling on Dale. Smiled the most evil, wicked thing Dale could remember.

The silence around them became tangible.

"I have just gotten off the phone with the Secretary," he cast his voice into that hollow space.

Spoken that way, there was only one person he could be referring to. Kyung-Hee Sala. Madam Secretary of the Interior herself.

The Boss.

The smile turned warmer by notches.

"I assured her that Mr. Embry's questions were the product of youthful exuberance, and not insubordination," Azad continued.

Snickers could be heard in the corners of the room.

"Still, she felt that some level of discipline was appropriate," Azad said. "Much less so, however, once I played her the tape of the General's briefing."

Azad turned and speared Stan with a knowing look.

"The whole tape."

Stan grinned, and shrugged. Dale still held his breath.

"Mr. Embry, you will write a scholarly analysis of the Posse Comitatus Act and relevant, associated case law," Superintendent Azad commanded. "The districts of the Rocky Mountain Front Command will consider using it as a basis of communications with the Department of War, going forward. We have two weeks before things get ugly on the border. I will expect it then."

He nodded to the three men individually, turned, and left without another word.

Dale remembered to breathe. It could have been much uglier.

"Careful," Wilson said into the stillness.

He was always a man of few words. Dale waited.

"They'll make you a lawyer if you aren't careful."

The room laughed.

Dale shuddered, unable to visualize anything worse.

Rustic Barracks was a small place. A few more than a score of wooden buildings at the eastern end of town, spread out across the narrow canyon and covering both sides of the Cache la Poudre River.

Dale found himself making one of his rare forays off of the base the next morning. It felt like afternoon, but that was because he had woken up at his usual four AM for breakfast, and then had to sit around reading his new biography of Ben Franklin for several hours before the library opened.

It was even weirder to be dressed like a civilian, in blue jeans he wore so rarely they were barely faded, a black t-shirt, and a burgundy chambray shirt over that. Only his cowboy hat was left over.

Ten AM was close enough to lunchtime. It felt like half the day was gone. But he figured the walk would do him good since he normally lived in the saddle.

Before the war, Rustic had been nothing more than a couple of resorts on the river and a base camp for hikers and adventurers. Now it was a Park Service town, providing support and entertainment to the Laramie Mountains branch of the Rocky Mountain Front Command. It threatened to turn into a town when nobody was looking.

As a result, the library wasn't contained in the Barracks anymore, but had moved further up the road along the frozen-over creek, past the gas station convenience store and the burger joint that Stan considered worthy of a Michelin Star, if only those folks would ever come visit.

Dale glanced at his watch as he got close, knowing he was still early, but the lights were already on inside and the door unlocked. He let himself in and looked around.

On the left, four computer terminals hard-wired to service from Fort Collins, and from there, the rest of the civilized world. On the right, tables and cubicles for reading. In the middle, a spot for the librarian, already occupied. All the way around the walls, bookshelves, with occasional windows and skylights.

Dale was shocked to see Cordelia Draeger in the chair, her crutches leaned against the counter, sipping fresh coffee from the smell.

"Mornin'," Dale greeted her with a smile. "Wasn't expecting you today."

Dale and Wilson had rescued her from a crashed sleigh nearly two months before, and she had kinda settled in around town since then. Well-liked and well-respected.

The only thing anybody nice had to say about the man that had made her a widow was that he was dead now, and had set her up with a goodly amount of money when she sold off all his gear.

After Jameson Hunt had bought her, and her debt-bond, from a brothel in Dodge City. On the Confederate side of the line.

"Hello, Dale," she smiled back. "What can I do for you this morning?"

She was pretty. Maybe the prettiest woman he knew. But she was way too old for him, thirty-two when he was about to turn seventeen. Safe enough as a friend, though. He hoped.

"Need to do some research for the Superintendent," he replied, moving to the clipboard on her counter to sign his name.

Dale could have accessed the web from a small cubby-hole back at the Barracks, but he preferred to stretch out and think. Plus, Azad had given him and Stan a few days off, and he wanted to be away from uniforms. Even Stan had understood, though he had promised to check in regularly and make sure Dale wasn't having problems.

"Anything good?" Cordelia asked.

"Old laws," Dale said, careful not to tell a civilian anything about an impending military operation. She didn't look like a spy, but... "Wilson's afraid they want to make me a lawyer or something."

She laughed outright. Musical. Warm.

"You'd be a good one, Dale," she grinned. "But you'd be pretty miserable."

"Could you tell them that?" he replied, leaning on the counter and relaxing.

She was wearing a heavy skirt and a wool sweater, both in shades of gray that went well together, with gloves on her fingers. There was a small electric heater near the desk, but it probably wouldn't do more than keep ice from forming on the insides of the windows for a couple of hours.

Cordelia smiled.

"I would ask if you need help finding anything," she said. "But I'm pretty sure you know where everything is better than I do."

Dale shrugged and nodded. Wasn't any *maybe* about that. He had spent more time in here since he arrived two years ago than any of the librarians.

"Anything I can get you?" he countered, knowing he was far more mobile than she was.

It had been a clean femur break, without any complications, but she was still going to be months fully healing. Might not go hiking in the mountains until late summer. Certainly didn't belong on horseback.

She just waved him off with a smile as she sipped her steaming mug. Dale nodded and walked to the computer terminals. In his granddad's day, they had come from China. After the wars and upheaval of the last thirty years, that stopped.

These days, they were made in Oregon. Still programmed in Seattle and San Jose, but Dale had no interest in more than just visiting the west coast of the Republic.

Today, he just needed them as tools.

The Coastal Republic had inherited most of the old United States Constitution, at least from a legal standpoint, a stack of historic precedent rollup with large chunks of English Common Law mixed in with frontier statutes from the late Nineteenth Century.

That included the Bill of Rights.

He knew from other things he had read that Posse Comitatus had frequently run headlong into the Third

Amendment, not because of what it said, but what the implications were.

How military rights were circumscribed by civilian control.

No Soldier shall, in time of peace be quartered in any house, without the consent of the Owner, nor in time of war, but in a manner to be prescribed by law.

Meaning: Civilians were superior to the army.

But how much so?

Dale began typing, and reading.

In *Youngstown Sheet & Tube Co. v. Sawyer, 343 U.S. 579 (CE 1952)*, Justice Jackson went further.

"Even in war time, [a military commander's] seizure of needed military housing must be authorized by Congress."

Ergo, the Congress of the Republic could order the Department of the Interior to do something, but the Department of War could not. Civilian control was the bedrock, both of the old United States and the Coastal Republic that had succeeded it. It was a sword that cut both ways, unlike the cavalry saber he hung from Centurion's saddle in the field.

In other cases, like *Griswold v. Connecticut*, those same underpinnings were used along with the Fourth Amendment to provide a basis of privacy for the individual. Again, limiting the power of the government, in this case the combined might of the military, from doing anything but what had been approved by the Congress, ordered by the President, and validated by the Courts.

A tap on his shoulder brought Dale up from the rabbit hole. He looked around, surprised. Cordelia stood next to him, leaning on her crutches.

"You've been in there for four hours, Dale," she said firmly. "It's time for you to take a break and get some food in you."

He blinked.

Four hours?

Sure enough, just after two in the afternoon. He looked at the notepad he had been using and realized he had half a dozen pages of tightly packed notes on it. And a rumbly tummy.

"Yeah. Okay," he said. "Food would be good."

Lord knows, he might go utterly feral, missing an entire meal. Growing boy, and all that, to hear Mom's words in his head. Dale smiled and rose slowly, giving Cordelia time to step back.

"Got plans?" he asked in a light tone.

"Yes," she replied. "Getting food in you. My shift is over and I'm hungry. Burger?"

That sounded like heaven. Dale held the door for her and then closed it up tight against the breeze. One of the other librarians had taken over, and a few customers had come in.

It was late enough that the lunch time rush had fallen off. Ademola's was supposedly the best burger joint, at least this side of Denver, if not in all of Colorado. Aruzhan Ademola, the woman who owned it, should have been cooking in Paris or someplace, to hear the old-timers talk.

Why she wanted to be here made so sense. Nobody's business but her own.

The place wasn't that small, but the smell hit Dale as soon as he stepped inside the door. His stomach positively growled in anticipation. He paused to let his eyes adjust, but Cordelia kept going and settled into a booth in the back. As Dale got close, he recognized Stan sitting there.

Cordelia, bum leg and all, had slid in next to Stan. Dale took the other side and let his imagination wander. Stan?

Cordelia Draeger might be the prettiest woman he knew, but Aruzhan's daughter, Aiman, was a close second. She gave Dale a pretty smile that made her bright blue eyes dance against her dark skin as she brought them glasses of water and menus.

Dale blushed and buried his nose in the menu, all flustered up. The way Stan grinned at him didn't help.

"So how goes the research, young man?" Stan asked, sipping his tea and far more relaxed than Dale ever remembered the man being.

He caught Dale's quick glance at Cordelia and nodded.

"In general," he continued.

Dale set his menu down, there really hadn't been any doubt what he would get, and ordered his thoughts.

"I've learned a great deal this morning," Dale said carefully. "But something Wilson said has me nervous."

Stan arched an eyebrow at him while Cordelia sat still and watched the by-play. Wilson might be the least talkative Ranger in the Service. Stan Hawkins was occasionally close behind him.

"He said they might want to make me a lawyer, one of these days," Dale said, trying to keep his voice from cracking with suppressed emotion.

"Nobody will *make* you, Dale," Stan replied. "But I agree that such an option will be available to you, if you want it. You have the makings of a good administrator, even a Deputy Secretary."

"I want to be a Ranger," Dale said. More than anything.

He'd wanted it bad enough to spend all of his time in the woods with his Dad, growing up; to press to be allowed to join the Service as an *090*, a Guide when he turned fifteen, and could pass the entrance exam with flying colors. And had.

"I understand, Dale," Stan said calmingly. "But you need a good education, even better than your Father and I have been able to give you. And more than you've gotten out of all the books you've read. You need people."

"Stan, I want the badge," Dale countered. "And Centurion and the wilderness. Nothing more. And I sure don't want to leave the mountains for four years."

Cordelia laughed. It was warm and funny, but more of a snicker at him than anything.

"Because four years is forever, right?" she said around giggles. "My God, you'd be twenty-two and *OLD*."

Dale held his peace. He'd kinda walked into that one. Stan had been a Ranger for thirty-five years, and Cordelia was already thirty-two. And neither of them were old.

Happily, Aiman came back for their orders and distracted him. Not so much that he didn't see the way Cordelia kinda leaned on Stan as they sat side by side, but Aiman had a heart-shaped, dusky face with such a pretty smile.

And he really wanted a double burger with bacon, cheese, and fresh avocado, cottage fries on the side.

He watched the woman walk away. Well, girl, he supposed, since she was only two years older than him, but still.

Stan was grinning almost as much as Cordelia when he turned back to them.

"What?" Dale asked, a blush suddenly working its way back up his face.

"Nothing, young man," Stan said. "We were talking about your research."

"Stan, I'm not sure it's worth doing," Dale replied. "I understand why, but I don't want to become a *303*. The Admin side has nothing I want. I wonder if I should even do this paper."

Stan's hazel eyes turned nearly gray as Dale watched.

"Dale," Stan said in a low, dangerous voice. "One of these days, you will be an Incident Commander with the Service. You might not believe me, but I know you. When called, you will serve, and do so with distinction."

Dale bit his tongue rather than argue with this man. He did not grind his teeth, but only barely.

Stan saw that and continued.

"You have a chance to leave a permanent mark on the Service right now, young man," Stan said. "To shape it for generations. I understand you not wanting to be anything more than a Ranger. I was the same way. I have turned down a promotion to Incident Commander. And they offered more than once. I would like to see you as the Secretary of the Interior, one of these days, shaping the entire Republic. But I also understand that it might be a door you don't ever want to walk through. I didn't. But I had the choice. You need to be aware of the consequences of your choices today, for what you want to be tomorrow."

He fell silent at that.

That might be one of the longest speeches Dale had ever heard Stan give, so he knew how much emotion the older man must have wrapped up in it.

Cordelia gave him a tight smile. Warm. Supportive. The

kind of thing one of his aunts might have done. Finally, she spoke.

"I know it's a bit of a secret, Dale," she said softly. "But I also agree with Stan that there are times we have to do things we don't personally enjoy, because they are bigger than we are."

She grabbed her glass of water and drank past what looked like a suddenly-dry throat.

"I have been there," she continued. "And I made some dumb choices when I was your age. The kind that put me where I was when you found me."

E.g. bought out of a Dodge City brothel debt-bond by a notorious liar and card sharp named Jameson Hunt, and subsequently rescued from sure death in the Colorado wilderness by Dale and Wilson when that same Mr. Hunt managed to get himself killed.

She and Dale shared a secret nod. Stan might know her story, but he hadn't been there to see those eyes when Dale lifted that chest off her leg and saved her life.

"If Stan Hawkins thinks it is a thing worth doing," she continued. "I'd be hard-pressed to argue the point."

Dale bit back his response to Cordelia, as well.

He knew they both meant well, and spoke with a breadth of experience he lacked for all of the military philosophers and experts he had read.

Dale would be seventeen in a few weeks. His mother had raised a hard-headed child, a driven one. He knew that. Had no doubts about it whatsoever. That determination had gotten him this far, to this place in the Colorado wilderness, breathing slowly and steadily as the pretty girl brought their burgers to the table and smiled extra warm at him again.

He just didn't want to do it. And nobody could make him.

Darkness.

A warm snap had come through the mountains, so the winds weren't viciously bitter outside. Avalanche risk would rise everywhere if it got too warm, but there was nothing dangerous in the immediate vicinity of the barracks.

Right now, it was the middle of the night, and sleep wasn't coming.

Dale let his unconscious feet guide him, out of the quad he shared with three other Guides, and down to the stables.

Centurion must have been restless as well. The big, blue roan stuck his nose up against the bars as Dale got close and slobbered on his hand.

Dale didn't want people tonight, even the ones in his head. He knew he had read more books than probably any three other people here, including Stan Hawkins and Hilar Azad. They were constant companions, offering advice, warnings, and support, from the Duke of Wellington, to Musashi, to Churchill, to Schumpeter.

Centurion seemed to understand. He moved back as Dale opened the stall door and went inside, insisting only on getting scritched under the chin and behind the ears, like normal.

They stood in silent tableau for an unknown bit, the smell of horse and man mingling. The sound of fingers digging softly into hair. The slobbering of a happy horse.

A footstep caused Dale to look up, drawing him back to the present from his wallow of self-pity.

Wilson.

He must have wanted to make a sound, because normally the man could sneak up on rattlesnakes.

"Thought I might find you here," Wilson drawled. "It's the place that draws us all. Home."

Dale studied him in the empty silence.

Six foot five. Big chest. The scrawny legs too many riders had from not walking enough. Blond hair. Clean shaven. Hard and silent. An archetype so many of the others might have been cast from.

"Talked to Hawkins," Wilson continued. "Miss Draeger, as well. Understand you're concerned."

"I know my duty, Ranger," Dale half-growled.

He wanted to resent Wilson, too, but the man embodied so

much of what he wanted in life. It would be like resenting the sunrise.

"It's not about duty, Embry," Wilson replied. "We all understand duty. This is about doing what's right."

"What's right?" Dale echoed, confused.

"The Army thinks about war," Wilson said. "They sometimes forget that they aren't always in the right, just because they don't ever question. If it moves, you shoot it. Simple enough. But why were you standing there to see it move? Not many people understand how important asking *that* question is. Hawkins does. I might, on occasion. You most certainly do."

"So I should ask those annoying questions, and that's enough?" Dale fired back.

"No," Wilson shook his head. "You understand that there will be people over there that are going to get hurt because of what we do. And nobody else will ask how we could have done this better. Nobody will push as hard as you to make the world a better place. *That's* what right is."

Wilson leaned against the door and fell silent. Dale joined him. Only Centurion made a sound, snorting occasionally as Dale forgot to scritch.

No, he supposed nobody would push as hard.

Dad hadn't raised him to shirk his duty. His hand had gone up. If you were going to say no, you had a responsibility to offer an alternative. Dale could suddenly see how many people were counting on him to do that.

He nodded to Wilson.

Wilson nodded back, turned, and vanished on silent boot heels.

Duty.

Nothing more. And nothing less.

Dale was at breakfast. He was incapable of sleeping past four AM, so all that was left him was to doddle in the shower, and get ready, and then eat slowly. Ben Franklin's biography awaited him, but he would finish it in another hour or two of reading.

All of yesterday had been consumed in typing his ideas into a computer here in the barracks library. He had been able to close the door to the small cubicle and work, uninterrupted for a whole day, emerging only for potty breaks and lunch.

Somewhere around eight PM he had saved the file and transmitted it to the Superintendent. Considering the final document, Azad might be one of the few in the Barracks capable of doing a good editorial pass on it, as so few of the others had the necessary historical and legal background.

The morning shift had been and gone, leaving the mess hall bereft. They would be mounted up and departing on patrol over the next half hour. Most of the admin staff wouldn't be up for a while yet.

The door opened, and the Superintendent entered. Azad spotted Dale, nodded, and went to grab some coffee. He came over and sat without a word.

Dale's plate was almost clean. But he still had half his tea to go. Azad placed his own mug on the table and rested his chin on tented fists.

"I read your paper last night, Embry," he finally said. "Went to bed and chewed on it all night. I had originally intended to transmit it out as updated addenda to the Rules of Engagement this morning."

"But?" Dale couldn't help himself.

"You have a way with words I was unprepared for," Azad confessed. "I have known a few cowboy poets. The Service attracts them. You have their gift. But you also have a very rare grounding in law and history. It makes a powerful combination."

He paused, expectant.

Dale wasn't going to bite. He'd gotten into enough trouble with the General. Azad finally nodded.

"I could order it, Embry," he said carefully. "But I would like to make it a request. Would you be willing to give this paper as a speech? The locals would appreciate it far more as spoken word. Too many of them would skip over all the good parts."

All the good parts? Did this mean the man liked it? Really liked it?

"And I would like to invite the General and his staff back, as well."

Oh, crap. So I'm to be the piñata?

Dale nodded carefully. *Duty.* Nothing more. And nothing less. His hand had gone up.

Azad seemed to see through him.

"Don't worry, Dale," the superintendent said. "We'll have them outnumbered."

"Yes, sir," Dale held himself to.

Azad rose and departed. Dale let go a heavy sigh.

The tea had turned to ashes in his mouth.

So this was what a last meal tasted like.

The room had not changed, other than Dale was seated in the first row this time, eyes focused directly ahead at the whiteboard as people came in behind him. He would have liked to have Cordelia here, but she was a civilian, and the coming attack would be discussed.

Wilson had surprised Dale by walking down from one of the upper rows and sitting next to him.

Silent as always, but as strong, as solid, as Mt. Rushmore.

Dale stole a glance back over his shoulder as the footsteps abated. It was hard to separate the lighter green uniforms of the Park Service from the darker ones of the Army, but there were a great many of both. And more along the walls and aisles.

Standing room, only. Literally.

Dale sucked a breath all the way down to his toes, like the Taoists and Zen masters commanded. Now, if he could just get his heart to stop racing.

Superintendent Azad opened a side door at the bottom of the auditorium and strode to the lectern with a smile Dale would have called simply triumphant, if pressed for a word.

Azad could be like that, a bantam rooster for such a small man, but today, he had it going in spades.

"Ladies and gentlemen of the Service, and honored guests," he said, pitching his voice to ring off the back wall in a manner similar to Stan Hawkins. "Thank you for being able to join us today. I had tasked one of our Guides, Dale Embry, with writing a scholarly piece on the importance of Posse Comitatus, as it impacts the relationship between the Department of War, and our own Department of the Interior."

Azad paused, holding every eye in the place in his hand. Dad had that trick. Dale had studied enough people see how it was done, but this was still exceptional.

"Rather than email it to everyone to be ignored," Azad continued with a knowing smile. "I have asked Dale to present it. I have spoken with the Secretary of the Interior, and this will be added to the Service's Rules of Engagement for this district, going forward. Dale, if you would?"

Dale rose stiffly, unwilling to glance back at the utter mob behind him. The room was built for one hundred eighty people. Right now, it probably held twice that.

He would not flinch. He would not falter.

Dale made his way to the lectern as the Superintendent took Dale's chair next to a grinning Wilson. It made an interesting contract, those two men, so unalike, yet seemingly drawing energy off of one another.

Dale pulled the folded pages from the pocket of his jacket and flattened them out on the sloped wood, still not looking up.

Piñata. Duty.

He took a breath.

The General was there, seated in the fourth tier, almost dead center. About six feet above him, forty feet away. His scowl could have been used to carve stone. But then the man relaxed that snarl into a friendly smile.

Dale watched him pull a folded printout from his own breast pocket and open it.

They locked eyes across the space, for just a moment, and Dale understood that the General had already read the speech, perhaps consumed it, before he had arrived. That the man understood every bit of it.

The General nodded at him, as if they were alone in the room, and mouthed the words, "Good job."

Dale felt a huge weight spill off his shoulders like an avalanche giving way.

Dad's training in public speaking came to him now.

He let his gaze encompass the entire room. Rangers and Guides, *025*'s and *090*'s, but also the *303*'s and *189*'s of the Admin side. What shocked Dale was the number of young officers the Army had brought. Perhaps two score Lieutenants and Captains, plus Majors and Colonels. And how many different unit patches these men and women had on their shoulders.

He wasn't here as a piñata. Azad had said so, not in as many words, but Dale hadn't believed him, hadn't understood the implications.

Dale was here representing the Park Service. The civilian law enforcement that would follow behind the Army, protecting the strangers who were suddenly on the wrong side of the line between nations.

Dale looked down and drew another deep breath.

"18 U.S. Code 1385," Dale began slowly. Cowboy Poet. "Posse Comitatus. *Whoever, except in cases and under circumstances expressly authorized by the Constitution or Act of Congress, willfully uses any part of the Army or the Air Force as a posse comitatus or otherwise to execute the laws shall be fined under this title or imprisoned not more than two years, or both.*"

The room had fallen utterly silent.

Maybe it was all the soldiers in the room. Park Service people were never that quiet, except in ambush.

"We are here today to discuss the importance of civilian control of the military, and demarcation between making war, and enforcing the law," Dale continued, feeling some unknown energy rise out of the people before him as he read. "But first, I would like to share a quote, of which I have taken a few, obvious liberties, to frame things more properly: *Thirteen score and seventeen years ago our fathers brought forth on this continent, a new nation, conceived in Liberty, and dedicated to the proposition that all men are created equal. Now we are engaged in a great civil war, testing whether that nation, or any nation so conceived and dedicated, can long endure...*"

REFUGE

D ale squinted at the green and white landscape of a western Kansas late spring, one long field of snow and grass that seemed to stretch out in front of him forever.

Wasn't it everyone's dream to invade a foreign country on their birthday?

He had seen the Army's preparations for this operation, this mess, so much more than that of the Park Service. They were huge. Far bigger than was justified. Hell, the western half of both Kansas and Nebraska were mostly abandoned these days, or reduced to tiny frontier towns, once you got past the forts guarding the frontiers themselves.

Partly, that emptiness was the end of trade between countries over the last few decades. But also, it was a fear of raids just like this one coming out of Colorado. Four columns of Coastal Republic troops and armor, moving like fingers, striking out to hit and occupy a range of civilian and targets from Garden City in western Kansas all the way up to North Platte, Nebraska.

With a large chunk of Colorado's Park Service, and Dale, behind them for law enforcement.

Emptiness, rolling across the western plains.

Secretly, Dale had a theory that the Confederate States really wanted was to keep their people away from the border so they didn't just up and leave for a better life in the Coastal Republic, or worse, get infected with modern ideas.

He could have told those politicians not to bother, but there was no helping some people.

So here he was, riding along a gravel country road atop his big, dumb, blue roan stallion, Centurion, in company with Stan Hawkins riding Audrey. The mid-day sky was cloudy and the wind a blustery chill coming out of the northwest, promising rain and threatening another late snow.

Somewhere behind them, right about at the border itself, was a convoy of 4x4 trucks and trailers that had gotten them this far, as the Service's Rangers and Guides spread out to make sure everyone behind the new front line was safe, from each other and the nasty weather coming.

Western Kansas was suddenly behind the army, for at least as long as the battle lasted. If not longer.

On the saddle, Dale's lever-action carbine hung from the right, and the saber from the left. On his hip, the old-fashioned cowboy six gun: six inches of steel barrel, single action trigger, .45 Long Colt rounds. Heavy, tough, durable.

Almost as much a symbol of the Park Service as the badge on Stan's chest and the patch on Dale's shoulder. The badge he wanted for himself.

One of these days.

Northeast Colorado had been rough country. Not impassable, just not flat enough to farm, even in the good old days, four decades ago, when this had all been one country. Before Drumph and his black-shirts. Before the Park Service led the Resistance. Before the war that got vicious when some idiot dropped a nuclear bomb on downtown Los Angeles.

Back when Stan Hawkins was only barely older than Dale was now, freshly minted as a Park Service Ranger, before things made them the law enforcement branch of the Coastal Republic. At fifty-eight, Stan was thought to be the final person still on active duty that had been commissioned by the old United States government.

Today, he was simply the Last Ranger, Dale's friend and mentor. And boss. At least until Dale stopped being an *090*, a Guide, and got promoted to *025*, Ranger.

One of these days.

Dale could see their destination ahead, through a few rough stands of trees and a strip of ponds along the creek. It used to be called St. Francis, Kansas, seat of Cherokee County, back when there were enough people around here to warrant such a thing.

Before some enterprising moron in eastern Colorado with a mean streak and a tailwind had set the wildfires that basically destroyed everything in this entire county as a civilized place.

Not many people had been killed, but the city had been

demolished. And being only fifteen or so miles from the front lines and the border, very few people had come back afterwards.

The few locals who called this area home referred to the place as Francis Corner these days. It wasn't much more.

The tiny airport southeast of town was generally abandoned. The local cathedral of the plains, a three-silo, concrete grain elevator on the forgotten old rail bed, was still there, but there weren't enough farmers these days to support it, so it was slowly falling in on itself. A couple of brick buildings and churches had survived to be colonized by the sorts of people who would live on such a frontier, mostly traders and get-rich-quick men. But mostly, trees seemed intent on using the shelter of the ruins to establish themselves. Not that western Kansas had many trees, other than the creek running up the northwest side of town.

He and Stan passed another burned out and looted foundation, saw the remains of a storm cellar across the old front yard. Nothing useful remained.

"This is why war is a bad idea, Dale," Stan finally broke the twenty minute silence that had wrapped the clomp of horse's hooves on dirt.

Dale glanced over, but kept his opinions to himself.

Stan nodded.

"Used to be, this was nice country for wheat and maybe cattle," Stan continued. "Now, nothing grows here but weeds and trouble."

Dale had to agree. Two centuries ago, the summers had been cooler and wet enough to support swamps like Cheyenne Bottoms in western Kansas. Hell, even two generations ago, before a few mild Dust Bowls a century after the big one, people could barely hang on. Now, the summers were desert hot and bone dry; and the winters cold, wet, and miserable, piling snow up on any vertical surface at sixty miles per hour.

Weren't many farmers at Francis Corner, these days. Wasn't a place for honest men and women to make a living.

"So you suppose they'll try to hold the land, this time?" Dale asked.

This was only the latest in a series of back and forths on the border over the last few decades. Denver, Boulder, and Fort Collins were all fortress towns. Safe. You could do that when it was possible to emplace really big artillery batteries up on very high ground with tail winds to loft shells into the teeth of any Huskers or Jayhawkers coming across the line.

On the other side, Hays and Garden City were barely worth the effort to defend, with all trade generally flowing eastward now, down the Arkansas River to Wichita and eventually the Mississippi.

"Not sure it's worth it, Dale," Stan replied. "Folks around here don't want us, so we aren't liberators come to save them. No real border terrain until you hit the Missouri River in Kansas City or the Flint Hills down southeast."

Dale was reminded history lessons and books about the marshes and steppes of western Russia, swallowing up European armies of conquest, whether Napoleon or Hitler. There was nothing until you hit the Ural Mountains in many places, or pushed until the locals had enough and pushed back.

Soviet Marshal Zhukov offered a few choice suggestions on the topic, but Dale kept them to himself. Stan might not even recognize the name, though he would have understood the tactics that man had used.

Dale shrugged instead. As Senior Ranger, Stan had the responsibility for Francis Corner itself, with Wilson covering the area north of town, on the way to Haigler, Nebraska, and both Deanna Okoye and Eskarne Obasanjo, two of Dale's other favorite Rangers, on the road east to Bird City and the new front line. Another barracks had everything south of them.

The ancient map called this River Street, coming in from the northwest through the creekbed of the Republican River, itself mostly a swamp of ice and mud right now. The remains of the grain elevator were on their right, and the one main road that was still intact ran down what used to be the front of the elevator.

Dale whistled at the shattered stumps of old homes and businesses to his left, like teeth broken off. The poet Shelley came to mind.

Look on my Works, ye Mighty, and despair!

From all that on the old maps, to just a general store, two bars, a brothel, and a few other businesses catering to the few local farmers and ranchers still hanging on.

Dale's favorite was the farrier. It was still easier to cross the land on horseback and wagon in many parts of the western plains, there being precious little budget or inclination to fix up old asphalt roads or patch gravel. And gas stations were rare if you didn't run on electric motors.

Dale wondered if this area had just simply reverted to the early Twentieth Century and would stay there forever.

Faces peeking out of windows got Dale's attention. He tried to smile and look friendly, but there was precious little happiness over there.

"And we're sure the Army disarmed the place?" he asked, counting the growing number of rough-looking men, and a few women.

"Any guns they could find, yes," Stan replied. "With an understanding that possession of anything but a shotgun after yesterday was probably a hanging offense. Borderers know the rules. They'll assume we're only here for a few days, and then gone, so they won't do anything stupid."

"One hopes," Dale countered.

"One hopes," Stan agreed.

Whiskey Rebellion was the larger of the two bars on the main street. People weren't spilling out the front door, but it was open and there was a small crowd inside, watching.

Not angry. Not even agitated.

Poised.

Stan pointed Audrey in that direction at a slow walk. Dale and Centurion followed.

There were already several horses tied to a long rail out front.

"You sit tight up here," Stan ordered in a quiet voice as they got close.

Dale reigned in and watched Stan ride close, dismount in one long, fluid movement, and drop Audrey's reins across the rail. She would sit fine, unless somebody got too close or too friendly. Then she might bite or kick.

"My name is Stan Hawkins," he announced in a clear voice that carried on the breeze. "I am a Ranger of the Coastal Republic Park Service."

Dale found his right hand near his pistol, but not on it.

Just careful.

Nobody seemed to be breathing over there.

The next building over was the brothel, and several women had appeared on a second-floor balcony, not that many feet above Dale, nor that far away. Some of them were even pretty, but all of them were hard.

Dale remembered how rigid Cordelia Draeger had been when he first met her.

Silence, all the way around.

"As long as we are here, I am the law," Stan continued. "Does this town have a mayor?"

"Here," a man's voice rang out. "Dan Simon."

The crowd parted to reveal the man. Dale was six feet tall and well built. Stan was taller and lankier. The Mayor was taller yet, and bulky, but it was the mass of what Dale's Mom would have called a German peasant. Three hundred pounds hanging on six foot four. Soft and kinda roundish.

Extremely well-dressed, though, in a suit that probably cost more than Centurion's saddle and tack.

Fancy.

Dale caught himself before the impish grin got to his mouth. Things were supposed to be serious here.

"Mr. Mayor," Stan said loud enough to still be heard. "I'm only concerned with crime that presents a problem to life and property. If you folks think you can manage everything, then Mr. Embry and I will generally stay out of your hair. If that ends up being a problem, we'll have to establish a permanent presence."

The way he said that last bit, as he turned and swung back up into Audrey's saddle, sent a chill up Dale's spine. From the looks on faces o'er yonder, Dale wasn't the only one that understood the polite threat of brutal violence under Stan's words.

But the two of them rode the rest of the way down the main strip in companionable silence.

Francis Corner would take care of itself.

Or they would.

The Support Services team had set up a camp a little southeast of Francis Corner, right next to the old airport stripe that was still more or less intact, if supplies needed to be flown in. Close enough Dale knew he and Stan could get there in a hurry, but mostly out of sight.

Any little thing to help calm these people.

Nothing had burned down last night, at least. And no gunfire that would draw them in. Stan had assured him that the folks over there needed at least one night to blow off steam.

This morning, they made their rounds slowly to give everyone time to breathe. Francis Corner had never been occupied, mostly just passed by as the war ebbed and flowed. Not important enough.

There was a light breeze promising a cold drizzle later, but it had held off all morning, despite the clouds overhead. Dale rode next to Stan as they came into town from the east, passing the jagged remains of what had once been a cute, little town, two generations ago. Not much remained, but Dale could see spots where locals had salvaged things to make other buildings.

Given another generation, the town might come back. Or it might not.

That wasn't his job, today. He was here with Stan to put the locals at ease.

Centurion and Audrey took up two spots on the rail out front of the Whiskey Rebellion Bar and Grill, along with two other horses not nearly as nice looking or well-trained.

Inside, the place was dim, but not dark. Atmosphere, rather

than need, since the roof was covered with enough solar panels to probably run everything in the village.

Francis Corner was too far removed from anywhere to be on a power grid. They had learned to make do.

Few locals were up, even as it was already past noon. Probably sleeping off last night's ruckus.

Stan had taken a spot in a back corner, looking out, with Dale on his side in the other corner, watching the bartender, who might be the owner, and the waitress, who might be his wife. They had that similarity that a couple supposedly got after decades together, both of medium height and rather stout, with the kind of complexion that suggested Greek ancestry rather than Cherokee.

She had brought them water and coffee, and left menus behind, smiling a great deal more when Stan showed a sheaf of Confederate Dollars. She wouldn't have to take Loonies and worry about converting them, nor be out the cost of serving the two Park Service folks lunch. Nor run the risk of denying them service.

"Will they convert the cash later?" Dale asked in a quiet voice.

"That depends on how things go on the front line," Stan shrugged. "If the Army holds. And if the locals choose to stay put. And a dozen other possibilities. But we absolutely need to be seen as the good guys here, Dale."

Stan paused to fix Dale with a close look.

"That's one of the reasons you and I are here," he continued. "Wilson, or the two ladies, Okoye and Obasanjo, would do just as well, but my name is known around here. I want yours known as well. That will be important, one of these days."

The woman came back at that point, cutting off any reply Dale might have made.

He settled for watching people as they came in, looked over at this corner, and scooting over to the far end of the place, or up at the bar.

Anywhere not too close to the Coasties.

The Mayor came in as they were finishing up their steaks,

Stan having splurged on t-bones and cottage fries today. Stan gestured for the man to join them.

The man still looked like he spent more on his clothing than his house. Food might be a close second, considering how overweight and soft the man was, though.

"How can I help, Mayor?" Stan asked, cutting straight to business, rather than asking about the weather, as was normal with folks like this.

The man was taken aback. Almost staggered before he recovered.

Dale made a note of how useful a tactic that could be, especially with a glad-hander like Simon.

"What do we do if there's trouble and none of you are around?" he finally demanded in a small voice after he caught his equilibrium.

"What kind of trouble would you expect?" Stan solicited.

"You tell me," the mayor fired back. "We're behind enemy lines now. Disarmed. At your mercy."

Dale watched Stan's eyes grow cold. Simon recoiled slightly under the weight of that glare.

"We won't ever be far away. You will be treated just like civilians anywhere else, as long as you behave," Stan said. "And we're paying Confederate dollars for our lunch."

"And what if one of you Coasties gets out of line?" the Mayor asked.

"Then they will answer to me," Stan declared.

Dale felt a chill down his spine.

A week of normalcy had passed.

Dale and Stan had fallen into a pattern with their daily patrols, walking through town once in the mid-morning, maybe stopping for food or coffee, and then passing through Francis Corner again late in the afternoon, giving everybody time to eat their supper and settle down when the headed back to camp as the sun slowly headed for the horizon. There would be one more loop in a few hours, just before sunset, to tuck everyone in.

Things had calmed.

Even the ladies of the night had settled back down after a few days, falling to business as the ranchers around the old county started to trickle back in.

Stan was reading in his tent. Possibly napping.

Dale was currying both horses, more for something to do than need. But the admin folks didn't mind sitting to watch him work, instead of him sitting to watch them.

A shot rang out of the purple dusk. Sharp and carrying in the still air.

Dale didn't even realize he was gone until he and Centurion galloped out of the camp with as big a head of steam as that blue roan could light under his ass.

Town was seven-eighths of a mile away, up to the old highway and then across, turning north at River Road to get around most of the ruins quickest.. Centurion flew like he could see in the noon sun, even as the sky overhead was fading. At least the Corner was well lit.

Eighty seconds later, Dale and Centurion rounded the north corner of the mausoleum that was the grain elevator at a dead gallop.

Dale knew trouble as soon as it appeared.

Out front of the bordello was a wheeled scout in Coastal Republic splatter green paint, with the eleven stars in a circle, representing the founding states of the Republic, on the side of the gun turret.

The doors on the vehicle were all closed, and the lights off, so Dale took a chance that the whole crew had disembarked before they started whatever trouble was coming.

He considered the cavalry saber on the left of his saddle horn, but nobody was on the street in green. And Stan had taught him to never take a carbine indoors in a tight situation.

He threw himself from the saddle as Centurion slowed, and let the momentum carry him up the stairs and onto the wooden sidewalk out front. His hand was on the revolver on his hip, but he didn't draw.

Not yet.

Instead, he put all his weight and his shoulder into the closed wooden door and jammed it as hard as he could.

Someone had locked it, which just meant that Dale's mass shattered the wood holding the strikeplate in place. That same someone had apparently been leaning against it, as well.

Hadn't done him any good.

He was on his face in the middle of the room, under the door, as Dale sorted everything out.

The Park Service used an ancient design for their revolver, but manufactured to modern specs.

Dale drew the heavy steel and thumbed the hammer back in one motion, holding the hammer with his thumb as he pointed the long barrel at the group of men at the far end of the long salon.

There was a dead man in the middle of the floor, face up, unseeing eyes watching heaven.

From his size and his clothing, Dale recognized the mayor. Looked like he had tried to step in when things started to get out of hand and had gotten killed for his trouble.

Nothing fancy about being a dead man.

Seven other men were down at that end of the room. Five of them seemed to be watching the other two having their way with one of the local girls right there in public instead of upstairs in private.

From the terrified look on her face, there was no amount of money they could have offered to make her a willing participant in what they had in mind.

And they didn't look like they had any intention of paying.

The four other girls along both walls would have stood no chance whatsoever trying to stop these men.

One of the men in a Coastal Republic Army uniform like the rest was older and had three chevrons on his sleeve. A semi-automatic pistol rode at his belt.

"Don't move," Dale ordered as the man spun around.

"What the hell do you want?" the sergeant sneered with a long SoCal accent. "The boys and me were just having a little fun, is all."

"I'm the law," Dale said in a hard, angry voice. "Keep your hands where I can see them and step away from the girl."

"My pants will fall down," one of the two men pleaded.

"I'm not really finding a lot of sympathy for you, right now," Dale countered.

His barrel was dead-centered on the sergeant as the men faced him. Tall. Burly. Blond. Sneering.

Perfectly still, though, so aware how little effort it would take Dale to pull that trigger. Very obviously not making any motion towards the pistol on his hip.

"So now what?" the sergeant mocked Dale. "We're the Army. You think you're just gonna take us in?"

"I can already name several sections of the UCMJ that cover this," Dale fired back. "That's the Uniform Code of Military Justice, since you gentlemen don't look like you ever bothered to actually read it."

The men grumbled, but nobody moved.

Dale's barrel wasn't wavering, even as butterflies started to multiply in his belly.

"These losers are Confederates," the sergeant replied. "They got it coming."

"They are civilians in a war zone," Dale let his anger surface, just a little bit. Like opening the refrigerator door in a dark room before he closed it again. "And I'm pretty sure you men belong in Hays, or somewhere, so you might also be deserters, as well."

"There are eight of us, cop," the man's voice turned ugly. "Your gun only holds six rounds."

Dale knew that. And he knew that this man would be the first one to die, even if the rest of them took him. He ignored the implicit threat.

He had volunteered for this duty.

The Park Service.

Nothing whatsoever was going to sway him from doing what was right. Not even his own death.

"What's it gonna be, boy?" the sergeant snarled, shifting his weight subtly forward onto his toes. "I don't think you got the guts to shoot."

"If I was a gambling man," a thunderous voice intruded from behind Dale. "I would have been willing to bet good money that young Dale here could easily shoot four of you before you overwhelmed him. And then maybe he beats another one to death with his pistol before two of you manage to get out of that room alive. Maybe not. Dale can be a mean bastard when provoked."

Stan Hawkins. The Last Ranger.

Dale took a deliberate step to his left and pivoted his body so he could peek back over his shoulder. His eyes were back on the dumb, California jock before the man could react.

Behind him, Stan walked into the room, pistol drawn and pointed at the soldiers. Deanna Okoye and Eskarne Obasanjo entered and flanked the man. Wilson brought up the rear, with his carbine tucked up against a shoulder and no doubts whatsoever in his eyes.

"You probably thought that Dale was here alone," Stan continued with a hard, jagged edge to his voice. "He's never alone. Just riding a bit out front, showing the rest of us the way."

"All of you, on your knees," Dale ordered. "I'm not asking and I will not speak again. Now."

"What if we refuse?" the belligerent sergeant countered.

Wilson was generally held to be the least talkative Ranger in the entire Service, so anytime he spoke, it had value.

"Then you die," Wilson replied. "Most of you are looking at five to twenty years at hard labor. That's a promise. Except you, Sergeant. I will see you hang for this."

Dale saw the hangman's noose appear in the other man's eyes, and knew that man was never leaving the room alive.

Everything dropped into slow motion.

The flickering in the eyes as the man made up his mind.

The sudden twitch that brought the right hip back and the shoulder down.

His right hand slapping leather as he wrapped one tanned-mitt around the butt of his semi-automatic and started to draw.

In the books and movies, things like this were always gentlemanly affairs.

Two men facing off on an otherwise-empty street and drawing as one.

Dale shot the man in the center of the chest before the sergeant could even finish his draw. And he had no idea if the man was wearing body armor under that uniform, so he put a second bullet into the man's brain about the same instant that the four Rangers behind him opened up.

The sound was comparable to the Apocalypse.

And over about as fast.

Dale drew the hammer back and pointed it at the others.

"Stockade or morgue?" he snarled at them.

The seven survivors fell to their knees with their hands in the air.

Dale glanced back.

"Thank you," he said to the foursome.

"Meant every word of it, Dale," Stan smiled back. "I'm proud of you."

Dale nodded. This was a year for firsts in his life, growing up in the Park Service.

And if that meant killing his own people to protect total strangers on the other side of the war, so be it.

They were the Park Service.

They were the Law.

ABOUT KNOTTED ROAD PRESS

Knotted Road Press fiction specializes in dynamic writing set in mysterious, exotic locations.

Knotted Road Press non-fiction publishes autobiographies, business books, cookbooks, and how-to books with unique voices.

Knotted Road Press creates DRM-free ebooks as well as high-quality print books for readers around the world.

With authors in a variety of genres including literary, poetry, mystery, fantasy, and science fiction, Knotted Road Press has something for everyone.

Knotted Road Press
www.KnottedRoadPress.com

www.ingramcontent.com/pod-product-compliance
Lightning Source LLC
Chambersburg PA
CBHW071447030726
47593CB00003B/928